CARTOGRAPHIES

Winner of the
Drue Heinz Literature Prize
1989

MAYA SONENBERG

Cartographies

UNIVERSITY OF PITTSBURGH PRESS

Published by the University of Pittsburgh Press, Pittsburgh, Pa. 15260
Copyright © 1989, Maya Sonenberg
All rights reserved
Baker and Taylor International, London
Manufactured in the United States of America

Library of Congress Cataloging-in-Publication Data

Sonenberg, Maya, 1960—
    Cartographies / Maya Sonenberg,
        p.   cm.
    "Winner of the 1989 Drue Heinz Literature Prize"—P.
    Contents: Cartographies—Quarry games—Nature morte—Seces-
sion—Ashes—Ariadne in exile—June 4, 1469—Interval—Afterimage—
Dioramas.
    ISBN 0-8229-3627-5
    I. Title.
PS3569.065385C37   1989
813'.54—dc20   89-31841
                                                                                 CIP

The author gratefully thanks the MacDowell Colony for support during the
writing of this book.

The following stories have been published previously, some of them in
slightly different form: "Afterimage" in *Grand Street*; "Cartographies" in
Gargoyle; "June 4, 1469" in *Columbia: A Magazine of Poetry and Prose*;
and "Nature Morte" in *Chelsea*.

For my parents,
my teachers,
and for John

CONTENTS

CARTOGRAPHIES

CARTOGRAPHIES

IT HAS ALWAYS been this way with the map-makers: from their first scratches on the cave wall to show the migration patterns of the herds, they have traced lines and lived inside them. After a meal of scorched meat and a few hours of fitful sleep in the smoky corners of the cave, they felt the antelope trot through their arteries, then crept out into the night and followed the tracks, so intent on the pursuit that they missed the hoots of the night birds calling to each other in the grasses all around them. In Babylonia, suzerains hired them to draw maps of fertile valleys with sharp sticks in clay tablets, showing the streams and the well-worn paths between the plots of grain. Then the scribes and planners dropped their sticks to follow the paths in single file or hand in hand in pairs. Ptolemy called for their assistance with his eight-volume *Guide to Geography*, asking them to copy neatly his list of 8,000 places. At their tables in the library in Alexandria, the names they scribbled called up wide expanses of blue water, the colored sands of different ports, the movements of whole navies across the Mediterranean, the flags flying at the boats' sterns, the cracked tooth in a sailor's mouth. In the New World, the mapmakers painted a plan of Mexico and a map of the gulf whose waters they had never seen. Montezuma gave these to Cortez so the conqueror could travel more easily from one island to another, from one tiered temple to the next, and, thus, charts facilitated the demise of one empire and the birth of another. Swords slicing easily through brown skin, Cortez's cavalry thundered through the jungle, and the mapmakers ran into the uncharted depths of the trees and vines to escape. In 1554, Mercator rolled the earth into a cylinder, coaxing it between his palms, sticky, like a ball of clay. As he spread it out flat, his apprentices watched the continents fall squarely into place. In themselves they felt the lines draw taut, parallel and perpendicular. Ever more accurate, maps are now made with the trimetrogon process. A plane flies at 20,000 feet, and wide-angle cameras photograph the terrain from horizon to horizon. Under the bright office lights, the mapmakers lean over and cast their shadows on a flattened world, photos that show the tiniest details—houses, cars, people, dogs—seen from above, bits of skin on the earth. In the future, they will watch from orbit, trace continents with lasers, and spin the globe on their computer screens. When the mapmakers walk out into the night, they walk out into the map, but the city has risen around them and the black buildings block their view.

"Imagine we visited Canada together," one mapmaker says to another. Her eyes sparkle in her still face. "Wouldn't you expect it to be pink?"

Across the glass coffee table from her, he is playing with his key chain, throwing it up and catching it again as it nears the gray rug.

"First we would see the Horseshoe Falls," she says, "all that blue water tumbling over the edge and shading to purple where the deep pink of the rock showed through. In our carnation pink slickers, we'd join the honeymoon couples and go down the damp magenta tunnels behind the falls. We'd emerge at the railing and catch the spray full in our faces. Through the gaps in the wall of water, we could peer across to the American side where everything would look green."

She watches the pale oval of his face tip up and down as he tosses his keys, and she extends her arm tentatively over the table. Her skinny fingers hover, flick away some soft dust that's settled on the arm of his chair, and she withdraws her hand. He pitches the keys to her and she flings them back as if the metal were hot, laughing. Jangling, the keys flash copper and leave red marks in their palms.

To make a map of your favorite mountain, climb that mountain, walk around it, follow the ridge to the neighboring mountain, look back at your mountain from above and below, walk back along the ridge, climb down the other side of your mountain.

Next, go to the nearest airport and hire a pilot and small plane, or maybe a helicopter to fly you over and around your mountain.

Take pictures from the air.

Remember all the details you've seen, the angles at which you've placed your feet, the places where it was so steep you had to hold on with your hands. When you get home, make a model of your mountain out of red clay, using the photographs only if you have to.

Flatten it.

He steeps himself in the maps he makes and thinks that they, in turn, are immersed in him. He thinks the coastline of South America overlies his liver, the streams line up along his veins. Cars travel his nerves as they travel the interstate, their drivers following the route of his thoughts. The oceans fill his abdomen. His muscles are the earth, and if he were to stroke his cheek, he'd brush the treetops of Tanzania. He takes the world printed flat on a parchment and folds it into his brain.

When he walks down to Washington Square, it seems the brick buildings have been pulverized, and the view is unobstructed. He sees the numbered side streets ranging north and south and the ordered avenues ranging east and west to the rivers where the ships are secured to the docks and the barges ply the waters. He sees other people also walking to the fountain in the square. Their hands are in the pockets of their loose-fitting clothes and their heads thrown back to look at the sky. Walking inward from Thompson Square, from Sheridan Square, from Madison Square, they follow the grid he follows, and he feels that as he walks he pulls them along. Among the others, he can see the woman he is going to meet. She wears dark glasses and stares at the ground, sensing where to turn rather than looking. She doesn't realize that the sky above her is blue, hear the trucks rumbling or the scattered car horns in the distance. Perhaps she takes the network of cracks in the asphalt and superimposes that on some other system of branching lines like the wrinkles under his chin, and perhaps she follows those lines in her mind as her body follows the streets. In his brain, all the people proceed to this center, the square, leaving their trails behind them like snails' slime: a map of the city.

In the park, men dance under the arch and lounge on the benches, but he notices only the woman standing by the fountain, her back to him. Against the white spray the outlines of her body are sharp; her dark hair, her tan legs and arms, her blue-and-black checked dress are like a paper doll's, she stands so still. He approaches, breathing quickly, wiping his hands down the thighs of his pants, anticipating how her body will take on substance as he touches the shoulder of her dress that's partitioned like the city. She may be startled, but he'll never know from her static face. She'll never know that, with his touch, he's just created her flesh.

"Imagine you're a sailor on the high seas," he says to her. Leaning back against the thin pillow, he clasps her hand with his, holding it tightly. His voice is hushed by the dark, muffled by the buzz of the air conditioner. "At night, you lie on the pitching deck which is hard and smooth and cold beneath your back. It's a dark night—no moon— and the smell and taste of salt is everywhere, as if sodium is the commonest element. But you're used to that; you barely notice it any more as you barely feel the wind that pushes you across the Atlantic or hear the creaking of the timbers or the slosh of water against the sides of the ship. These things have become constants. Above you the stars are out, bright dots, hard to look at, hard to hold on to, but if you stare long enough, you begin to see faint lines between them like those you've seen on the maps—constellations.

"You're a young sailor learning to navigate, hoping to rise from sail hauler, knot tier, deck scrubber. You are learning to read maps. The one of the stars presents few problems. It's just a matter of recognition and memorization, for you can imagine spreading the night sky out flat on a table; it's not a matter of faith. Navigational charts have become this for you—a matter of faith. They baffle you. How do you know those soundings are correct? How do you know some island and its surrounding ledges and shallows will not appear in front of the ship one night, unforeseen? You tell yourself that you must trust the map, the mapmaker, the navigator who has traveled this ocean before, over and over you tell yourself, but you're still not sure.

"As you lie on the deck amidst coils of rope, you try to imagine the corrugated contours of the ocean floor—the Mid-Atlantic Ridge, the Canary Basin—as you saw them in the blues and browns of the topographic map that was unfolded, its creases flattened, on the table. You wonder which of those formations you are many fathoms above now. They say there are mountains down there as tall as the Rockies or the Himalayas. You wonder what good that map of the ocean floor does for you except that, should the ship go down, you'd at least know where you were. If the wind were to rise suddenly and bury the ship under a wall of water, you might be able to give the fish directions to the Sargasso Sea. But it wouldn't happen that way: you scare too easily. Pretend to be in control when you're not. With your eyes closed, you'd keep reaching for the mainsail line long after the mast had snapped.

"Trapped between two maps, moving along the grid of a third, you lie there on the cold deck.

Parallels run east-west; meridians run north-south, you tell yourself with the stars swaying above and the water below."

The blanket traps their heat, and she moves to throw it back. His arm, though, lies across the quilt, a weight like a string of pearls around her neck. She sits up, frees herself from the tangle of sheets, and his hand slides down to her lap.

"You can't sleep," he says, reaching toward her back, the ridge of her spine running neatly down the center.

When she stands, she slips into the cool air as if it were a satin robe, stretching her arms, flexing her wrists at the ends of the sleeves. "Obviously."

She turns off the air conditioner, opens the window, and hot air drifts in with the sweet smell of exhaust. Leaning on the sill, chin in her hand, she watches the traffic light switching red, green, red, and a man running under the streetlamps with his dog. Their steps ping-pong over the metal basement doors, bouncing up the street.

Through the window the light spills around her, puddling on the floor, and the fronds of her fingers curl toward it. She rocks slightly. He was buoyed up by her body and then sank, pressing her down under him with the heels of his hands.

When she turns back to her room, the other mapmaker is sucking in his stomach, buttoning up his pants. Shadows fall around his white body like bars of sunlight running through water.

If he can read the maps of cities, the maps of stars, of seas, of sedimentation, he can also read the map of the human face. He has memorized the charts of thought and feeling that compartmentalize the face and label the distortions possible in each quadrant. The other mapmaker—she's the one exception to these plans. The nerves to the surface muscles of her face are damaged, and she can neither smile nor frown. He can read the damage in her constant calmness and in the scars of her numerous and ineffective operations where the doctors peeled back her skin as if they were peeling fruit. At times he tried to read her eyes, but he soon learned that it is the muscles around them and not the whites, irises, and pupils themselves that give expression. And those muscles are isolated in a wilderness without roads. Her features are no key.

With her, it's all much harder work. He must ask and she must answer; she must speak and he must listen. The landscape is between them, but he thinks that she has an unfair advantage, a watchtower at the border from which she can see it all. He thinks she should be able to take him to the interior, to show him the country, following the dry streambeds and the deer paths that only she can see, that she should know him as easily as she knows the color-coded words on the maps; *his* face isn't damaged. He does not believe that she finds his face as hard to read as he finds hers. "My darkest Congo," she calls one cheek; "My uncharted plains of Kenya," she calls the other. "My Amazon Basin" is his chin; "My Antarctica," his mouth. "My Nile Delta" is his brow; the silt of his too numerous thoughts floats down and settles there, muddying the waters so she cannot see the rock formations at bottom slope into the sea. When she strokes his face with these names, she feels only the smooth, dead surface of a map. Softly, she asks him, "But what do you mean? I didn't know you ever needed to pursue me," and he repeats, "I'm not pursuing you any more." He says it thickly. Reaching up to brush back his hair, she slices her finger open on the sharp paper's edge. From the almost invisible cut, the blood flows freely, startlingly red, and she bends her head to suck it dry.

The forest is between them. They both approach it so cautiously. Like pioneers intent on staking their own claims, they cut tangential swathes through the trees. When they meet in these dark woods, they do speak, but the words are often jumbled, lost among the cracking branches, the squawks of birds settling for the night. They stand, lean on their axes. He spits out the grass stem he's been chewing and asks her about the trees. "Yes," she answers, "just like the ones by the fountain in the park." But if they were to look up, they would see trees so tall that their trunks squeeze the space between them to a point. Birds too far away to be seen from below steer between the branches and battle a fierce wind that can't be felt on the ground.

In the living room a table reaches from one wall to the other, white cloth dipping to the floor, candles poised in their holders. The two map-makers are giving a dinner party together.

"You're here already," she says as she swings into her apartment, back pressed against the door. He's sitting at the kitchen table with the darkness closing tightly around him like a glove. She can barely make out his features. Flicking the light switch, she watches him squint those earth brown eyes flecked with green. He has moved the chair from its usual place, shifted it to the diagonal so that he can rest his feet on the other chair, the one facing the windows.

While she slices dark green scallions on the white counter, he sets the table. First he walks around clockwise with a stack of plates on his arm and places one in front of each chair, making sure they are evenly spaced. Then he arranges wine glasses and water glasses to the right of the plates. He lines up forks and knives so their prongs and blades face off across the cloth, places salt and pepper shakers in pairs at both ends of the long table. Above the plates he lays silver teaspoons down so that all their oval bowls point in the same direction, circling the table like a line of minnows hanging suspended in a stream, like the dotted boundary line surrounding a state.

When she comes in from the kitchen, wiping her damp, red hands on a towel, the silverware shoots stars through the glasses. She laughs at the teaspoons though. He places the last one down carefully, straightens it, measures the distance between it and the plate with his thumb.

"That's not where you put the spoons," she says. Hugging him tight, she lifts one and places it to the right of the knife. "That's where it goes." She kisses him on the cheek and reaches around to untie her apron strings.

"No. You're wrong. They go across this way." He settles the spoon back in line, little silver bowl holding the light.

"Now, whose mother gave dinner parties for the mayor?" she says, crossing her arms.

"And who worked in a fancy French restaurant for three years to put himself through school?" He picks up the spoon and shakes it in her face. When he leaves the room, the glasses whine against each other. The bedroom door closes; he starts the rush of water for a shower.

Sighing, she lays the spoon down again next to the knife. It looks decidedly better there: balanced—the two forks to the left of the plate, and the knife and spoon to the right. But is it worth an argument? she thinks and puts the spoon back where he wants it. Perhaps it would look right there if they had more silver—three forks, soup spoons and sherbet spoons as well as teaspoons, a butter knife for everyone. She stares at the teaspoon, how it lightly bridges the cloth between two glasses, then lines it up next to the knife again. After a moment, she sweeps them all off the table and takes them into the kitchen. We'll just bring them out when it's time for dessert, she thinks.

To make a map of your favorite mountain, look at other maps of the mountain. Copy whichever you think is the best. When you copy it, add a number of different colored stars and a key to these colors in the margin. "From here, you can see my house in the village below." "Here is a flat sunny rock to picnic on." "The water from this spring is especially sweet." And so on.

You've made the map your own.

Next, climb the mountain, taking with you a number of large colored-paper stars. Follow your map and place the colored stars at the designated spots. Or, if you want your map to be inaccurate, place the stars several yards further up the mountain than you indicated. You've now made the mountain your own.

They sit in the sun, drink bitter coffee on which a milky film has formed. "Yes," she says to him, "there's always the problem of Greenland. There's really no way to get rid of it. Don't you remember learning about it in elementary school even? It's part of the curriculum, part of how you learn what a map is. The teacher says, 'See how the northern part of Greenland, the part that's covered with a glacier, is stretched out? See how much smaller it is on the globe? That's because the longitude lines have been spread apart as if the earth were a cylinder.' The teacher explains how those lines which seem parallel on the map actually curve around a sphere and join.

"There are solutions for this problem, but these solutions tend to throw the rest of the world out of kilter—the oceans cut up like orange sections, the shrinking of all areas not directly around a pole. We could have a clear picture of Antarctica and of nothing else.

"Don't you think that if you were to walk around Greenland using a world map as your guide, you'd have to walk very slowly so that you could mirror the sense of immensity suggested by the map and yet stick to the confines of the land itself? You'd stomp around the inlets and capes along the coast, map in your hand, but they'd all seem wrong, attenuated somehow. On the pier of a fishing village, a young woman would realize what your trouble was and give you a map that showed only Greenland, was centered on the island. You'd refuse at first, of course, wave her proffered bit of paper away, but finally, reluctantly, you'd accept her help and start off again, hopping from rock to rock. In a little while you'd realize that no matter how accurate your map was, the land mass would seem immense in relation to your body. You'd be walking forever." She pauses, noticing how his body is locked tense, leaning forward, and how he's watching her mouth. He looks the way he did the one time he saw her cry, his eyes rummaging in her face. The tears slid over her cheeks like water over stone. "Do you think you can get away without saying anything? " she asks and rises, dropping fifty cents to the table to pay for her coffee. The silver coins bounce on the white surface.

She steeps herself in the maps she makes, and they in turn are immersed in her. She absorbs them, internalizes them, whole cities inside her. When she was a child, she played the globe-spinning game with her friends. One of them gave it a push, and then all closed their eyes, rested a dirty finger on the colored surface, and waited for the globe to stop, the friction warming their fingertips. Then they opened their eyes and took turns describing the places their fingers had landed. They told stories about phosphorescent sea monsters that glowed beneath the surface before rising up to devour ships, about a thousand-foot-long snake that took a fancy to a small village, about head hunters who looked for replacements for their wives' heads which were the size, shape, and color of artichokes, about trees as tall as the Empire State Building with whole towns built among the leaves. Outside, kids raced relays in the yard.

She still plays sometimes. Waiting for the other mapmaker to show up, she spins the globe and lets her finger trail. She remembers visits to certain European capitals and envisions others. One night, Notre Dame springs up, flying buttresses cracking apart her living room floor. On the plaza in front, girls clump over the cobbles in their black clogs. She wanders inside where the candles burn steadily.

When the other mapmaker walks into her apartment from the cool evening, he finds the watery smell of the Seine, the smell of wax. She is curled in a corner of the couch, counting to herself in French. She tells him that in Paris the bees were hovering over the honeycakes in the bakeries, that on the street corners the boys swung their hair out of their eyes, that in the cathedral the choir was practicing "Amazing Grace."

"Suddenly in the middle of the bridge to the Left Bank, I realized that everyone was speaking English. In my high school French I asked a young couple why, but they didn't understand me. They just looked at each other and shrugged their shoulders. They walked around me. No one noticed I was mumbling to myself."

He hopes to lull her, to quiet her descriptions of the narrow streets she didn't recognize, of how it was getting dark and she was reeling, hearing the strangeness of her own tongue. He makes her talk about something else, but he keeps catching her hands that scrabble at his chest and placing them firmly in her lap. Soon, her fingers begin to crawl and scratch again as if she were trying to climb a stone wall in the dark.

"I saw you on the street," she says. "I called out, but you didn't seem to hear." From the office windows, they watch the storm dump rain over six miles of city blocks. The clouds are dark green; the edge of clear sky in the west is purple.

"I've been away," he says, "a little vacation."

"Then I looked again, and I couldn't be sure it was you."

He spreads his fingers apart, hands flat on the glass. "On ancient maps," he says, "the ocean's far reaches are guarded by dragons. The mapmaker's home at the center is clearly delineated while the perimeters are hazy. If you were to visit those outer reaches, you'd find yourself slogging mile after mile through fog, slush, and mud. Around you, you'd sense the movements of the local inhabitants, oblivious to your daze and distress, to the squelching sounds your rubber boots make in the brown mud as you pull one foot free and then the other. You'd think of voracious beasts that could crush you as they rolled over. You wouldn't be able to see them clearly but only glimpse shapes through the fog.

"As the mud thins to dirty water, the fog lifts and you have a clearer view of these other inhabitants ranging up and down the coast to either side of you. They stand up to their haunches in mud, billowing their white breath, extending their scaly whiplike tails and their many-clawed forelegs, pointing their toothy snouts into the wind. Inside, your heart beats faster and you think of escape to a vaguely remembered shingle beach, but the fog still hides both the sea and the land. You stand still, hoping to avoid attention, but they've seen you. They lumber toward you, moving slowly, and each step sends shock waves through the mud.

"You remain frozen as they come closer. The fog lifts some more and you relax and release the breath you've held. They are only men dressed in many layers of animal skin. They've been pulling their boats in toward shore and billowing white breath with their exertion. That's all. You realize you've hit this country at a change of season—the air warm and the water still frigid so the moisture condenses and forms fog. You're on the shore at low tide in an area where the ocean floor slopes gradually down. These mudflats stretch for miles before the waves lap at them. It's all familiar.

"The men come closer, waving oars and harpoons in greeting, but their faces coalesce into grimaces. They stare at your yellow raincoat, mouths dropped open, as if it were the slick skin of a giant amphibian. On your unresponsive face they cannot read your fear. They can't hear your heart, but you can hear their grunts as they close in, lowering their weapons. The open water is visible now, and you rush in its direction, no hazy edge at all, just the deep, deep, cold, gray sea."

It's gotten dark. His voice wanders off, whispering. She's backed away and her heels patter on the floor. In the glass, he faintly sees her fumble to turn on the lamp. The bright circle of light surrounds her as she straightens her stacks of white paper, taps her pencil against her palm. He slides his hand over the cool surface of the window until it lies on her warm, round shoulder. Gently, he strokes the glass. From her desk, the light spreads to his back, fingers the hairs that curl over the pink collar of his shirt.

To make a map of your favorite mountain, figure out the shape that emerged from the crashing together of the tectonic plates many millions of years ago. Calculate the effects of wind, water, walking, and lumbering on the land. You'll have to know the airflow patterns, precipitation patterns, vegetation patterns, the history of human settlement and industry, as well as the properties of the mountain rock.

Your calculations, scribbled in pencil, will cover sheets of paper, the backs of many envelopes, the margins of a newspaper, and they will look nothing like a mountain.

You know how to turn your calculations into diagrams and how to get the vectors to mold the space on the blank paper.

Still, no mountain appears until you take the dare and trace its shape, faintly at first and then with bold black strokes.

"Let's drive to the mountains," she says to him one day in October as she wanders from room to room, looking out at the rows of windows across the way, all neatly curtained, and the towers disappearing into the sooty sky.

"Next weekend OK?" he asks, rustling his newspaper and glancing up to see the way she nods delicately and leans against the window, holding the curtain aside.

Their first morning in the country, the two mapmakers get up early while the sun is still pale on the colored leaves. At the foot of Mt. Lincoln they open the car doors and the cold air shocks them, penetrating their clothing as they stoop to lace their boots. They start hiking, walking quickly to warm up.

Clearly marked with blue blazes, the trail is easy to follow but much steeper than their map suggests. It twists up the mountainside and they must often use their hands to pull themselves up. Dirt fills the lines in their palms. The trail crosses a stream back and forth and proceeds through a gorge so narrow it forces them to walk in the water itself, rushing past them, ankle deep. On their map, the stream curves gently down the mountain, a blue line that meanders several yards from the trail.

"Maybe this is the wrong trail," she pants as they climb and climb, their thighs tightening and aching. "Or the wrong map." She holds out a hand for him to grab; he pushes her up an especially steep boulder in the middle of the trail.

"No, no, no," he reassures her. "It's a new map and here's the South Face Trail—right here— marked with blue. That must be what we're on."

Their mouths and throats are so dry that it hurts to breathe and there's nothing left in their water bottles. They scoop cold water from the stream, but it tastes rank like rotten leaves, the fur of long-dead animals, the summer's dust. On their map, the key promises good drinking water, a spring up ahead in a clearing. Watching the ground closely to avoid roots and sharp stones, they climb toward it, the image of it in their minds.

Three-quarters of the way up the mountain, she crumples the map and pushes it to the bottom of her pack. "There's no clearing with a spring. We might as well stop here," she says. They sit down on a rock and eat their lunch, savoring the oranges, while the golden leaves fall all around and land in their hair. He swings his legs, letting his heels knock against the stone. It is the only sound, and she can feel the rhythm match the knocking of her heart. The valley below lies still in the sun. Through it, a river reflects silver, doubles back on itself, and twists its way between a gap in the mountains to another valley. It reflects the hawks wheeling from cliff to cliff, crisscrossing the valley, and circling the mountaintops, a pattern of brown flecks like dirt. Their feathers fall, float on the ponds in the backyards of the village.

From the rock overlooking the valley, the mapmakers follow the blue blazes to the summit that's barren above the tree line, another hour's steep climb. They must stop every few minutes to catch their breath. At the top, the land opens up, unwraps itself before them, and they turn and turn to see it on all sides. At first they notice only the shapes of the hills rolling down to the roads and up again, following each other off into the distance, fading from the reds of the sugar maples variously turned to hazier and hazier blues. The sun slides over the solids and sets the colors floating.

As the mapmakers watch, their vision sharpens until they see the waterfalls tumble rock over rock like racers running hurdles, a whirligig spinning and flashing yellow on a lawn far below. In the clear air, woodsmoke from a fireplace hangs in dense brown shapes that constantly change. The golden light radiates from every point in the blue sky; it encircles the mapmakers on the mountaintop and spreads over the dimpled, pocked, and folded earth, over hills unnamed, marked but nameless trails, villages too small to make the map where women peel carrots for soup and young girls drift idly from house to house paying their calls, letting the bushes slap against their hands as they walk.

As the afternoon sun slips away, houses lose themselves in the folds of the land, streams disappear between the trees. The hills shift in the failing light. The mapmakers can only stand open-eyed and watch; they are unable even to stutter. Like the coming together again of the continents, the re-forming of Gondwanaland, they feel their bodies line up against each other. She feels that, as her arm winds around him, it circles some stone from the Precambrian period. Through the layers of wool and cotton she feels every muscle, every bone—rock formations before they were riddled with fossils. With his wide, smooth hand he passes over the side of her body, the hills and valleys of a forgotten land. He feels the coursing of underground streams and senses the stillness of underground lakes. They resist speaking to each other or calling out over the valley because, in Gondwanaland, the mountain ranges had not yet been named.

QUARRY GAMES

AT THE TOP of the abandoned quarry, Tommy waited for me, calling back over his shoulder, "Hurry up, Sarah," and I emerged there into the blasting heat that beat through the layers of the atmosphere and rebounded off the pink and gray stones. Breathing the dusty air, we surveyed our playground. Before us the uncut ledges fell away in steps, one of them wide as a plaza, and the slabs of granite lay where they had tumbled seaward through bush, bracken, and rusted machinery, block after toppled block. Beyond them the mud flats and the marsh with its dozen sunken bulldozers stretched out into the bay. Nearby, a truck was parked and a boat docked at the wharf.

As we stood pointing to the green pool hidden among the stones and to the scattered cables and sections of pipe, the wind came up off the water and blew the sun's heat from Tommy's head of dark hair and my blond braids, from his skinny arms and my narrow shoulders. We shivered from the cold. Tommy wrapped his arms around himself and I hopped up and down to keep warm until the wind dropped and settled the sun around us again under the hard blue sky, the tilting ladders of the cranes, the guy wires looped from post to post.

From our perch at the edge of the first cliff-like step, we had a view of the sea stretching to the distant, sharp horizon. Close to shore, greens and violets mottled the blue, but out beyond the shoals and channels the water was sequined with gold.

"Look," I cried, pointing. "Look how the water's reaching toward that line."

Tommy shaded his eyes with his hand so that he could see the rock and swell of the waves. "With each swell it stretches further," he said.

"As if it's reaching for a rope that someone's thrown."

Tommy's hand dropped, and he turned to me. "Oh Sarah," he said, "it's just water. It moves in and out and in again because of the tides. You know that. It's not reaching for anything."

"But the men reach into it to pull fish out like out of a barrel," I said looking up to him.

"No. Not like anything."

I still saw the water in all its blue-gold glitter grappling with the edge. But he might have been right. After all, he was older. I shifted my point of view as you can do by looking first through one eye and then the other. Through the other eye, the sea lay still, inanimate, and the glitter was only the sunlight reflected in the crest of each wave. I could see the water move at its edge, washing over and over the same stretch of shore. But it stroked the pebbles so softly, so gently, repeating the caress.

While I watched the sea, closing one eye and then opening it and closing the other, Tommy was already moving down the rocks to the smooth-floored plaza. I followed, picking my way and sitting to slide from stone to stone.

Down there between the cliffs it was hot. The floor was littered with granite chips and leaves, and on one side it opened to the sea. I ran across the expanse, my red sneakers sending up puffs of white dust, to catch up with Tommy who ambled along the edge, trying to find a way down to the shore.

"Tommy, stop. You can't leave. It's the day of a dance," I said. He looked at me blankly as I took his large hand. His long fingers wrapped around mine, and I pulled him back toward the center of the space. "It's our pueblo. See the adobe buildings. There are the doorways like black holes and the ladders leading from terrace to terrace. We have to get ready." From the dark doorways a song echoed out over the water, and a steady drumbeat filled the air.

"That's the desert out there at the foot of our mesa," Tommy said, pointing out to sea. I barely looked at the tumbleweed blowing over the dry ground because I'd started to hop and shuffle around the plaza in a circle, dividing the drumbeats into twos and then into threes and fours, dividing the beat also with my voice. I tried to hum along with the other voices, and Tommy joined in too. I sang the few repeated words of the song until they seemed to slip out of my mouth on their own. Tommy followed along behind me, swaying when I swayed, spinning madly when I stamped my foot and twirled. There was no one to call to us from stoop or window to tame the wildness of our steps.

We spun small circles along the larger one, and

with each spin the sandy buildings and the gray-
green trees whirled by. I felt the hot sun prick the
skin on my arms, felt it burn through the blue and
yellow feathers that fluttered on my dress with
each step. The dust and bits of blue down stuck
to my neck. When I turned, I could see Tommy
swinging his arms and the sweat rolling down
them, shining on his bare chest and sticky on his
face. The muscles in his arms rippled like water
under the skin. Though our voices grew thin, we
panted the tune out between breaths. We sprang
from side to side, letting our bodies flop and
scribed our circle tighter and tighter around a drill
hole in the center of the plaza. I felt myself rising
on the beat and, during a turn, I saw the hair radi-
ating from the crown of Tommy's head. With the
air spongy beneath me, I danced round and round
until my feathers, each a tiny weight, pulled me
down, and I stood solidly on the ground, cough-
ing from the dust we'd stirred up and watching
Tommy dance around the plaza alone in the hot
sun, his gestures small and repetitive like a wind-
up toy's.

The dark shapes of the pueblo doorways slid
across the stone, arranging themselves into
stripes, and the pattern papered the granite walls.
Loose blocks of stone grew backs and arms, and
then soft cushions sprouted in the corners of
the couches. The scattered leaves we'd shuffled
through stuck to the wide floorboards, dried spots
of paint. The pueblo was my studio and Tommy
my model.

"Freeze," I cried and he did, pigeon-toed, his
arms extended and bent like a bird drying its
wings. I began to trace his dark shadow on the
floor with granite chips. Bending over and careful

not to mix his shadow with my own, I let the chips fall through my fingers and bounce when they hit the ground.

"Let's go for a swim," Tommy said. I dropped my stones with a clatter. He had broken the pose, his limbs fallen together. Running off, he left me with his unfinished outline. I skipped after him, but he was already struggling down the slope through the thorn bushes and boulders to the sea.

It wasn't hard to catch up, and soon I was behind him. We squeezed between the granite blocks, climbed up them, and leaped from one to the next. Tommy led and pointed out the loose stones to me. Still, when I landed, I often disturbed their balance and felt the rocks move under me, tipping and sending me out into the air. But always before I fell, Tommy caught my arm and righted me again, his hand circling closed above my elbow, his grip painfully tight. I had red marks on my skin.

From building block to tumbled building block, we jumped. "People still live in them," I said as we passed, and I called their names, "Ralph, Fred Johnson, Sharon, Simon, Mrs. Jones." The mothers' dark eyes and the children's pale eyes rolled from left to right as we squatted, stepped from stone to stone, and steadied ourselves with our hands.

"Who are you calling to?" Tommy asked and crouched beside me. The Johnsons retreated into the dark, but they left their door open, letting us peer into their foyer where the dust lay in the corners of the black-and-white tile floor, where the jackets hung from the coatrack, and into the empty living room beyond where the television hummed a cartoon, the colored characters jump-

ing and screeching on the screen. As on all long
Saturdays, we were left alone to watch them, the
house large and quiet around us. A cloud passed
over and the screen went dark.

"Your family closed their door," Tommy said as
he stretched tall beside me. He ambled off, but for
a while I stayed, calling random names and rap-
ping with my knuckles on the stone.

Tommy faced the bay that sparkled below at the
foot of the quarry and sniffed the salt and the sweet
smell of dried grass that floated up on the air. When
I reached the point of the tilted slab where he stood,
I turned and looked over my shoulder, and instead
of a rubble of bricks, beams, and cornices, I saw
stone laps and limbs and heads.

"Look," I said tugging on Tommy's sleeve.
"Quarry giants only come out in the afternoon."
With their stone hands, they grasped at the passing shadows that fell like coverlets, and their
thick lips curled. Knocking the blocks of their
bodies against each other, the giants began to roll,
but they stopped, their rough-rimmed eyes opened
wide in pain. Like the sisters in the story who all
slept in one bed, they'd tangled their chunky legs,
knees bent back at odd angles, square calves
twisted under their thighs. My father had told me
how the three sisters' mother had to whack the
covers with a stick one morning so that each of
her daughters could grab her own feet. I giggled at
their contortions and Tommy laughed too, but
once the last cloud disappeared, the rocks were
still.

We turned to the water again and the scars of
work and then went swinging down between the
blocks to the thick net of bushes and the shacks
by the road. Behind me I could hear rumbling

laughter that began softly like the rattle of a few small stones tumbling down an incline but soon burst loudly from the rocks, cackling, subsiding, and sounding again.

From above, the bushes had appeared to be a green, waist-high barrier along the dirt road where it ran by the wharf, but once we left the last slab behind, we found a wall of thorns that snagged my shirt as we passed, ripping one of the seahorses on my sleeve. Alders reached far above Tommy's head. Parting the branches, we stepped through and let them close behind us. We could no longer see the water ahead or the toppled blocks behind, but only the muddy ground now and through the leaves, the sky, as we followed the slope to the shore.

Pushing the last rough twigs aside, we emerged, not near the wharf as we had planned but at the edge of the marsh where the dozen bulldozers squatted to the tops of their wheels in the muck. I sloshed out through the water and dried grass while Tommy sat on a rock at the edge of the woods, turning his hands red with a rusty link of chain.

From one earthmover to the next, I waded, brandishing whips of marsh grass. I cracked the dry grasses in the air and practiced my favorite songs, but the beasts sat dumbly and would not move. Up to the empty seats, I clambered and kicked their hard sides with my wet sneakers until my heels burned. I fiddled with their controls, twisting the knobs and shifting the levers that weren't stuck tight with rust. Though I yelled until my voice was hoarse, I could not enlist Tommy's help.

At first he blinked his round eyes like a cat in

the sun, sat up and started to rise, but then he slowly shook his head. "Get down from there before that thing collapses around you," he said, and he lay down again.

His belly rose and fell as he breathed the low-tide marsh stench that I had avoided by breathing through my mouth. I tried the air also—that smell of salt, rotten grass, decomposing shell-fish—and by the time I reached shore, I'd come to relish the smell that seemed to be the smell of my own hair and skin.

I dribbled water over the bridge of Tommy's nose and poked him until he sat up. He stretched sleepily in front of me. I shared his rock, letting my toes dangle toward the mud. Together, we stared seaward and I began to sing, tunelessly, a song my mother used to sing, and beat my feet against the stone in time. "Hush," Tommy said. He put his arm around my shoulders, encircling me, pulling me toward him, closing me off from the bay, and whispered in my ear how the rocks were hard and the mud was soft, how the water was cold and the sun was hot; he whispered in my ear until I no longer tried to squirm from his grip.

In the silence of the steady heat, we sat soundlessly suspended and still as if we'd been encased in some soft substance that cradled our limbs. My hands rested on the rock, tips of my fingers pink and casting circular shadows that shrank as the sun slowly moved. One by one, sounds returned—the slaps and gurgles of the waves as they hit the mud flats and withdrew, the rush of wind as it brushed the leaves together. We heard the men hollering from the dock down to the boat and the wavering song on their radio, tinny and distant, and we turned landward again to the ruined quarry. From below, we could see how the tar paper shacks rocked on their foundations, how the doors hung loosely open and the swallows darted in and out of the broken windows. The vertical post of the derrick tipped precariously, ready to collapse.

On the ledges, the men picked up the compressed-air hammer drills, made holes in sets of three, and drove the iron wedges into the rock so that it fell away in great slabs with a crash and a rising cloud of dust. The cranes swung the slabs down from the cliffs to the barges waiting at the dock. The clang of iron hammers on iron wedges rang from the cliffs where the men worked hard until the evening when they brought pokeweed and wild berries to the women in the big yellow house in town.

I closed my eyes and saw the yellow house on Main Street with its porches, balconies, and towers. I saw the men walk up to the door with sweat stains on their shirts and their caps in their hands. Tommy said that the women were locked into their turret rooms all day and had white skin like creatures from the bottom of the ocean where the water is black. The women thought the men's skin felt rough, like the side of the house where the paint was peeling. I saw the couples taking turns dancing delicately over the flowers in the parlor carpet and playing the same record over and over on the phonograph. Instead of talking to their partners, the women turned their heads and looked over their shoulders just as my mother did in the photo on my dresser: her glossy black eyes stared out of the frame while my father, holding her in his arms, stared intently at her ruffled, white sleeve. The men and women waiting held their hands out in front of their bodies and, tilting their heads together, compared tan fingers and white palms. The dancing couples stopped. I opened my eyes—just the granite blocks in the sun, the leaves spinning, the sound of the radio coming from the wharf.

Picking ourselves up and balancing on the slippery rocks, we walked down to the dock to watch the fishermen working. They filled baskets with fish from the boat and hoisted them to the square white truck, its ice slowly melting and dripping to the dirt. Lifting basket after basket high on their shoulders, they weighed and then spilled them so the fish fell in long, silver streams like mercury in the sun. In the darkly stained baskets, the fish overlapped, pressed around each other with their fleshy gills gaping open and their fins shooting out like rakes along their backs. Their eyes stared wide, the lenses clear and firm like semispheres of glass. If I picked them up, I'd find the slippery bodies surprisingly firm; I'd stare straight into their eyes, ask for wishes, and knowing the wishes would come true, throw the fish high in the air so they'd land with a splash, sink, and swim away, first purple shadows beneath the surface and then gone. "Come on," Tommy said, but we stood with our hands jammed tightly into our pockets, hypnotized by the weighing and spilling of fish and by the men's harsh voices and laughter rolling over the song on the radio and following the blue-green swells out to sea. The men ignored us—a boy, and a girl leaning against him, down the dock, watching and listening although we could not understand what they said.

I stared until Tommy took my arm and pulled me away. We backed down the dirt road, his hand still clutching my wrist, and when we could no longer see the men, we turned and walked quickly to the top of the quarry, then sat, swung our legs over the edge, and stared out to the horizon. We began to toss stones and to listen to the hollow sounds they made when they landed below, the way they rang on metal and echoed on stone. Once all the small rocks within reach were gone, we wandered back down the shady road and watched the dragonflies, their needles of color settling on the leaves, and I remember thinking that's all there is—the bright blue spliced to the green.

NATURE MORTE

IN PARIS IN 1911, the first cubist baby was born to an unwed mother from Avignon. She gave birth to him on the plaza in front of the tan buildings of the Louvre under a typically gray Paris sky. She was a large angular woman, the planes of her thighs, pelvis, and breasts meeting sharply. She made no sound as she lay flat against the gray ground. Picking up her child—not the squalling squirming thing that most newborns are but rather still and pale—she had trouble holding on to his amorphous body that took on the colors of his birthplace. She felt, as she walked away, that his many-angled body fit easily against her own and then again, that he grew or shrank and, suddenly, that her baby had far too many elbows.

I came to Paris to bear my child. Life in Avignon was too stifling, too traditional. The birth of a fatherless child there would have been scandalous. Yes, it was quite proper to have lovers, to have them bring you flowers or silks or chocolates. Yes, it was quite proper to receive them in your bedroom as you lay smelling roses, eating candies, to receive them in your broad arms. I could not have had my child there though. These trysts, although known by all, must remain secret. The links in the society must remain well lit, sharply defined. All edges must be sharply drawn. There was only one proper way to have a child in that society. You must proceed through a period of chaperoned courtship to marriage to the proper man, one of your own social class and in possession of a long and distinguished family history. The period of gestation was watched over by the masters, and these old men and women of the family trained you in their methods of child rearing. They taught you to make sure your child obeyed and reflected the rules of the society.

Hey, I saw this weird kid at school today. He was just standing there trying to fit in or maybe get lost in the crowd, but God, he'd just never make it. He was flat, or no, just when you saw him from the side or back. He looked real skinny then, but from the front, well, it was almost as though you could see all of him. He was wearing all brown and tan, or maybe *he* was brown and tan, but anyway, it was all patches sewn together with black thread. His arms—wait, I don't know if he had arms. Yeah, I guess he did. They must have just been hidden in all those folds of material. His arms and legs were sewn to his body, or maybe there was material connecting them like bats' wings. I don't know. I couldn't make him out at all.

He traveled often. The threads tied him to his birthplace, fitting snugly between the cobblestones. His tan settled into the wood of trees in Mesopotamia; his specks of green, the first shoots of wheat. He fled to Lake Chad in its unnamed infancy, and it reflected the blue of his mother's sky over Avignon or over a tryst in Barcelona or Le Havre, Assisi or Aix-en-Provence. Before, he fled to the moon, his threads absorbed by the wires in the electric circuits of the spacecraft, and ended up at Chartres listening to monks chant and Prokofiev's *Scythian Suite.*

My son, perhaps it was a mistake to send you out alone to be viewed and criticized, my son with a hundred hands, a hundred flat palms. "My boy," I said, "they tease you because you are different." He could not see this at all but perceived only his own pain. My son, you thought as we did.

Was my mother's womb filled with the flat blue water of the bay of Marseilles? Was she fed by her lover on irregular apples and oranges from the slopes of Mt. Sainte-Victoire? Was I conceived in one of those square orange houses surrounded by green trees?

In Paris in 1911, the first cubist baby was born. This occurrence, on the plaza in front of the Louvre, went largely unnoticed. I happened to be visiting the museum with my family at the time and, glancing out the window, witnessed this strange birth. A tall, dark-haired woman walked across the courtyard and, near the building entrance, lay down and gave birth. She appeared to be in no pain or discomfort although it was a cold cloudy day, and she was lying directly on the stones. As the baby emerged from between her broad thighs, I caught a glimpse of a brownish amalgam of lines and planes. Being a doctor, I was intrigued by this child. In twenty years of practice, I had never seen anything quite so strange. Neither had I ever read anything about a deformity or aberration like this in any text or journal, and I saw my chance to make my mark on the world. If I could expose this child to the scientific community after discovering the cause of its deformity and studying the effects of this deformity on its life, I would be able to contribute something to human knowledge, as well as distinguish myself.

My son, perhaps it was a mistake to send you out alone to be questioned and criticized, my son with a hundred palms, with a hundred symbols to be read. You wear these enigmatic signs: a bit of tomorrow's newspaper and a composer's name stenciled on your sleeve. "Alone?" you said. "My thoughts are solid companions."

My father created me in unknowing passion; my mother was a harlot of Avignon; I was conceived unwittingly. My father grappled blindly with the planes of my mother's body. He knew my mother well and was well versed in her ancestry, familiar with her family's origins in Egypt and Greece. He followed them through the churches of Constantinople, the palazzos of Italy, and the cathedrals of France. Each angle of my mother's body, the recesses of her elbows and knees, consolidated the limbs of her forebears. My father studied the details of the lines around her eyes. With her hair, he playfully covered her breasts and exposed them again. He followed the development of her leg and belly. He planned my conception as a step in a series of experiments, one of many children. My parents deciphered their genetic codes and found the strange compatibility which would produce me. They knew the right time for their union was at the moment of forgetting after years of study. My father created me in unseeing passion; he felt my mother's flat cheeks blindly.

As the woman wrapped the baby in her coat, I hurried downstairs. She was passing out of the courtyard and on to the Rue de Rivoli when I caught up with her walking slowly, as if having a baby should in no way disturb her stroll. I grabbed her at the corner. "Excuse me," I said. "I was upstairs and saw you give birth. May I see the child?" I was very excited and did not bother to explain the reasons for my interest, but this did not disturb her. "This is my first child," she said as she pulled back the folds of the coat. I gasped. I had never seen a baby so deformed, almost unrecognizable as human although I could make out traces of an eye or mouth on several of its many facets. I offered the woman a home and a living allowance for her and her child if she would allow me to conduct several simple experiments on the baby and observe him until he matured.

My body masked my words. People were always surprised to hear intelligible sentences emerge from my shifting body, my body with its suggestion of human features. My words mask my body. People do not look at me when I speak. My body masks my mind, this amalgam of planes and lines. This body is ebony. It is hard protection.

The woman refused my offer. "I did not leave

the masters of my family to serve the masters of science," she said, and I lost touch with them until she happened to bring the child to my office for his vaccinations, mentioning something about traveling far away. From then on, I observed him secretly as he was growing up, always hoping to be the first one to break the news though I never had enough evidence. He developed all the interests of a city-bred youngster and seemed barely daunted by the fact that he could never fully participate in the activities of his peers. He adopted all the beliefs, desires, likes, and dislikes of his generation.

This kid—the one I was telling you about—he talks just like us. I mean, it's a little disconcerting not being able to see where the voice is coming from, but it's all right if you don't look at him while he's talking. He's got some kind of strange accent—French, I think—but we were talking about baseball for a real long time. Seems he moved to New York from Paris. Of course, he can't actually play baseball. When he picks up the bat, it just comes apart in slices or multiplies in the air or something. But if he manages to hit the ball, then it's really unfair to the kids on the other team, because it seems like before he's even started to run, he's back at home plate, and so they voted not to let him play. He acts like a real New Yorker now. He keeps saying how '69 was the year, when the Mets won the Series.

His world is solid. He breathes in space that solidifies as it approaches. His body forms planes of space and flesh that adhere to the walls, to the window panes, and to the floorboards. Air hardens between his limbs, between his torso and his extremities, between his body and the cup he holds, the book he reads, the people he meets.

For some, he was too erratic. He grew too quickly or too slowly. He took care of his mother in her old age before she took care of him in his infancy. He spoke of distant lands and times as if he had firsthand knowledge of them or had studied them very well, but he was only a child who was never absent from school and was taught the bits of knowledge that all children are taught. He had strange fantasies about the future, about traveling to the moon or distant planets, about weapons that produced energy as the sun does. He could tell the story of his society; he could tell many other stories too; he could tell stories of places or events that had only an inner working order of their own. His mother's masters, the old women and men who had instructed her in the proper way to raise a child, thought him unsocialized. He could not comply with their tastes; he could not reflect them; he could not fit his amorphous limbs into the forms of their clothes and, so, often went naked. His father was very proud of him.

He watches his own birth from the second-story windows. He clings to the walls, the floor, binding with the air between the double panes of glass. "A bit of black blood," he thinks, "or maybe Spanish. I thought I saw my father once in Barcelona. In the twisted shapes of the Gaudi cathedral, I felt most at home." The baby, an amalgam of planes born of a strong gaunt woman, mingles with the gray cobblestones in front of the Louvre and Beaubourg; it mingles with the striated paving stones of the

Spanish sidewalk; it mingles with the interlocking roots along the African jungle floor, with the interlocking branches of the olive trees near Aix. His mother wraps him in his coat and carries him away.

SECESSION

IN THE CONDENSATION on the laundromat window, Colette draws stick figures that prance across the glass. She concentrates, giving them eyes that float near their square heads, connected by long nerve fibers, eyes that are too large, out of proportion, no mouths. One figure raises its hand in greeting, another doubles over in pain, and a third lifts wrist to forehead in the melodramatic gesture of a Hollywood starlet. Then she wipes the pane clear with her sleeve. Her cats have gnawed tiny holes into the body of her sweater, rubbed their white and orange fur into the green. She rests her head on her hand. Through the space she's cleared, she can see a few wispy clouds in the pale sky and the shop across the narrow street. The ceramic saints are lined up in its window—Mary in blue and Francis in brown, hands pressed together. Next to them, the milk glass flower vases and the candy bars collect dust. Clothes thud in the washing machines behind her.

Joseph led Colette through the aquarium. In the

43

dark spaces away from the lit tanks of seawater, he took her hand. As he read the signs out loud, he leaned down, his graying head next to her dark one. He liked planning these trips for her, taking her to places she hadn't visited since she was a child. When they stopped at the whales' tank, the thick glass felt cool against Colette's cheek. Around the corner a woman crouched next to a little boy and pointed, her finger a white dot pressed to the glass. Through the water her face was the wide, creamy unfolding of a peony. They were watching the whales too, watching the big animals spin easily underwater, watching their white bodies rise up to the blue-green surface and dive.

"See that pair," Joseph said. "They're taking turns protecting each other. They're playing," he added when he saw her looking for the danger and wrapped his arms around her, very warm.

The whales called and whistled, sighing, rough like gears grinding, then a high-pitched keening sound. On the other side of the tank, the red pom-pom on the boy's hat seemed to waver as the animals stirred the water with their weight. His mother's lips opened as if to let bubbles escape, as if she were singing sweetly and hollowly with the whales.

"Let's just stay here," Colette said. "We don't have to move." She heard Joseph humming in her ear, whispering things no one else would laugh at.

When I reach the red door, I'll stop, the round knob smooth and hot in my palm, and the wind cold on my neck, tugging at my hair. The red paint will glisten as if it's wet; it's all I'll see. Inside, at the end of the dark hallway, there is another door, and on the other side of that, my three bags will sprawl, toppled together, waiting for me to load them into the car. In the morning they lay open on my bed beneath the gable, and I packed them, saying "Colette, take this and this; you'll need them." Behind me—I'll turn and look over my shoulder, sun on my cheek—the sheets will be strung out on the line to dry as they are every summer, fastened with wooden clothespins, the white rectangles glowing, folding and flopping in the wind.

Colette fills the space in again with her breath and turns back to the rows of washers and dryers. If she weren't doing her laundry, what else would she be doing? At a long table in the middle of the room, an old man folds his clothes, and a woman sits at the far end, smoking a cigarette and turning the pages of a magazine. She brushes her long hair behind her shoulders. Across her back, the intricate cable pattern of her sweater expands and contracts as she breathes.

Going from dryer to dryer, an attendant unlocks and empties the change boxes with a jangling of keys and drops the quarters into the pocket of her blue smock. With each opening door, Colette sees the flames raging behind the machines. They shock her. She waits for the glimpses of a fire that's like orange hair blowing, like a face about to speak with a round black mouth. Skin constricts her lips. She taps her nails against the washer she sits on—quick brittle sounds.

Over her shoulder, the woman looks at Colette, and through the cigarette smoke, her features seem familiar, but when she turns to watch a car pass, her profile is not familiar at all. As the car

swings around the corner, a dog leans its head out
into the cold and, paws on window ledge, lifts its
chin to bark separate sharp sounds. The woman
turns back grinning, lips curled over her teeth, and
claps her hands, laughing silently.

When the rink opened, two boys were the first
to skate onto the ice. One moved forward slowly
and the other faced him, sculling backward, turning his toes in and then pulling his heels together
again. The sleeves of their parkas slid down and
hid their hands. As they skated around the edge of
the rink, the one moving backward kept flicking a
strand of hair out of his eyes. Two mauve scars
curled and crawled on his cheeks.

After stretching her legs along the rail, Colette
joined them, skating to the center of the ice where
she began to practice her figures. She twisted into
a three-turn, then leaned over and read the line
she'd scratched, checking to see if the cusp where
she made her turn was a clean, sharp V. Her blade
had kicked up a ridge of snow, and she pushed off
again, trying to hit the balance point under the
ball of her foot so that she would swing around
freely and leave a trace in which she could see her
own head held high and her back straight.

Back and forth now, the boys sliced figure
eights, turning quickly so that their skates beat
the ice. Their arms punched the air as they zig-
zagged across the rink, and their wild animal
shouts followed them. Colette thought how she
had first learned the serpentine figures, her
father's big hands letting her go, then steadying
her again. She'd learned to shift her weight just
slightly—her fingers spread in case of a fall—to
shift from one edge of the blade to the other.

While she drew the forms sure-footed now, no wobbling, the figures were still off-axis, wrong.

The old man rolls his T-shirts together with his flabby hands and piles the dingy squares at the bottom of his plastic laundry basket. In her lap, Colette twists the ring on her finger, the small diamond, the ruby and the pearl, yellow stripe of gold, until it chafes her skin. She wonders how much you can tell about a person from the way they fold their clothes. While the woman reads, her cigarette has burnt to a slender tower of ash, and Colette waits for it to fall, for the woman to brush it out of the crease of her magazine quickly with the side of her hand. At home, the woman will put the clothes, hers and her husband's, into the deep drawers of the rosewood dresser. She'll lay his shirts out on the bedspread for ironing. In their living room, the sofa is pale blue, and she'll lie back on it with tea and a file from work until the man gets home with the child and says briskly, "Why are you reading in the dark? Your tea's cold," so that she pouts and rises to make dinner, taking the child with her.

Suddenly the woman stands, very tall. She tugs her sweater down over her hips before pulling her clothes from the dryers and dropping them on the table, plumping the pile of jeans and socks and cotton sweaters and turning it, digging down deep into it with her long hands. Her face hard fossil bone, she looks right through Colette.

On the line, the sheets will be evenly spaced, strung from the white wall by the red door over the grass to the lilac bush, two wide ones for my parents' bed and two narrow ones for my own

hung out to dry, to be folded and carried upstairs
as if I'll sleep between them that night. Mother
will lie under the covers, alone in the house, while
I, while I. . . . On my bed, the sheets will lie slick
as ice while I. . . . Inlaid with gold, the leaves will
smolder as if the sun's inside them, and the white
sheets will flap against the brilliant green of the
trees and grass, luminescent.

Sometimes as they moved from one group of
friends to another, someone reached down to
touch Colette gently on the top of the head.
From her spot on the floor, she watched their
shoes stepping off to the edges of the room. Her
mother's red high heels were reflected in the glass
door leading to the dark terrace, and the men
pressed their flat feet into the carpet, first one foot
and then the other, their laces pulled tight and
tied into neat bows. The grown-ups' words fell, as
if consonants and vowels were running down her
neck, and their conversation sounded like the
refrigerator humming at night; always, before she
opened her eyes, she thought it was her father
whispering sternly to her mother in the next
room. Now she recognized his shiny black shoes
near her. His voice rose and fell, and a woman
responded, tipping the pointy toe of one shoe into
the air and sinking the sharp heel further into the
blue carpet, nodding and smiling. Her voice was
soft, each word small and round. Louder, Colette's
father laughed. When he stopped, he heard the
rattle of the small plastic blocks his daughter was
playing with. They cracked as she snapped them
together in her lap, her head bent over her work.
She was building an intricate, twisting wall that,
instead of circling around her, kept branching off,

insisting on splitting like a family tree. He heard her talking to herself, barely audible, but when she looked up at him, he looked away.

As she made her pattern, alternating colors and shapes, Colette said to herself, "Now it's green's turn and now it's yellow's." But she thought how she could trip that woman up so that she'd lie with her feet in the air like a dead bird. She crawled off, the woman's words rolling after her. She'd continue her wall on the other side of them and took a fistful of blocks. Instead, she went further, dropping one small block into each trouser cuff she saw, slipping them between the folds of cloth without anyone noticing. Later, when the men folded their pants over a hanger the way her father did, the colored pieces would fall out and the men would wonder where they came from, what message she was sending.

Under his loaded basket, the old man's back sways, his corduroy coat swinging open. As he opens the door, he huffs and sighs, stops to rest the basket on bent leg, letting in a wedge of cold air. When he gets home, he'll probably dump his clothes into his always open drawers or onto the cot by the radiator, his one room dark behind the green shades that he never lifts. Colette slides from the washer she's been sitting on and paces between the table and the machines. Joseph folded T-shirts so carefully they could have been silk, and then flung his clothes off at night as if ridding himself of a burden.

Without taking her coat off, Colette lay down at the foot of the bed, arms outstretched, palms to the ceiling. She looked up at the white washed gray with the rainy light, at the brown stain in the corner. When she came in, she closed the door firmly behind her, but now Joseph creaked it open. It made her dizzy to see his face upside down, his black eyes blinking slowly. She lay still, a dark symmetrical shape on the pale spread. He lay on top of her, lined his arms up along her arms, grasped her hands with his. "I guess I said something wrong again," he said. "You used to laugh when I kidded you; now you never respond." He sighed, kissed her cheek, but still she couldn't answer. Through all their clothing, his hipbones grated against hers.

Late at night, she woke, tenderness choking her, raised herself on her elbow to look at him sleeping in the dim light that leaked through the curtains. The two broad planes of his back emerged from the covers. He hugged the pillow with both arms. Stroking his cheek—that was the only thing that let her keep breathing for she could time her breaths, one breath for each stroke. With her fingers she touched his lips, open but silent. He was hushed, subdued, all his features gone slack. In the morning, he'd complain about not having cream for the coffee and joke about the way she dressed for work, easing the panty hose over her calves. She'd joke too, pretend to stretch the hose over his head while he laughed, but she'd half-wish him warm and quiet as he was asleep, a perfect form, the bridge of his nose shiny in the glint of light. He didn't even make any noise when he breathed.

He stirred, rubbed his eyes. "Could you get me a glass of water?" he asked sleepily. Her breath felt hot on his temple. Then he watched her shape shift, roll out of bed and go to the kitchen, turning the lights on in the hall. She moved so delicately, stopping to shake his raincoat and hang it up to dry.

Against the soles of Colette's feet, the floor was chill and she hurried. Things took on strange forms in the dark, Joseph's clothes tumbled like ghosts in corner chairs, but with relief, she saw the bright white light illuminated the same well-sponged counters, the dappled linoleum floor she had waxed that morning. When the cold water splashed and spilled over her hand, she brought the glass to Joseph. He looked up sheepishly as he gulped. Against his tongue and the roof of his mouth, the water was icy, and he felt it in his throat and stomach, still cold. Colette waited for him to finish, then put the glass away before returning to bed.

Already asleep, Joseph faced the wall with his knees drawn up tightly to his chest. She circled him with her arms, but he didn't move. She whispered in his ear, the sound of the radiators hissing.

"There are ways, my dear, to live with a man without suffocating."

Colette didn't look at her mother. She lay her hand flat on the pink linen tablecloth next to the wide white soup plate and traced around her fingers with a steak knife. In the vases around the room the flowers were rotting; they dropped their petals like slugs. Waiters hovered in the doorways.

"So tell me how," Colette said, looking up. The light was steely around her mother's head. Her mother's face was ridged, the wrinkles running down her cheeks and the powder caught in them like sand. The scars from her face-lift glinted white; they'd stretched as the skin sagged, slumped again from forehead to chin in drifts.

Mouth stuck in the middle like a gash. She just stared at Colette, thinking, "This is my child."

"Well?" Colette said. "The way you lived with Daddy? You two never said a word to each other unless someone else was around. Barely saw each other. Fucked once a month in the dark."

"Colette!"

"Now that he's dead, you don't have to deal with him at all." She was still holding the steak knife, gripping its wooden handle, pointing the tip of its serrated blade across the table.

"At least it was better than the way you live with Joseph. You don't talk to each other either; you just breathe down each other's necks and fight all the time. You never leave off gouging at each other. I don't see how you can stand it. At least we left each other alone." As she talked, she pleated the tablecloth in her lap and smoothed it out again. "Now, will you put that knife down, please. It's making me nervous."

The dryer clicks, clothes tumbling to the bottom of the drum. When Colette opens the door, the heat pulses up her arms and she drops her clothes on the table in a heap. The woman makes room for her, looks up, smiles. Her eyes sit close together, the chalky blue of mussel shells beneath the purple. She folds eiderdown covers, shiny with a basket weave pattern, and does the buttons at the open ends, her red nails jumping in the cloth like sparks. Her pillowcases, too, are of fine soft cotton, pale colors, and button at one end. Pursing her lips, she works briskly, efficiently, matches up the corners, gives the cloth another quarter turn.

She doesn't stop to question, Colette thinks— but she can do that herself and creases her towels sharply, quickly, with her hot hands, smacks the squares into piles. When she glances over and meets the chips of the woman's eyes, she speeds up even more. Her hands sprint in the sultry air; her hair sticks to her temples and she pushes it away. Grabbing her small items, her socks and underwear with the sagging elastic, she shoves them into her laundry bag. She will finish first, will turn to the other woman and cross her arms over her chest, lift her chin triumphantly. When she looks up again, the woman just smiles, calmly and openly as before, and stops folding clothes to comb her hair back with her fingers.

Colette's mother drew a thin line of glue along the base of the spiky lashes, then pressed them firmly to her own lids. She lifted her eyes and smiled at her daughter's reflection in the bathroom mirror. The room smelled of sharp perfume, and steam vibrated from the radiator under the window, stirring the ruffled curtains. Colette swung her legs so that her heels thumped against the side of the tub. In the mirror, her mother's chest shone above the white lace slip, the faint shadow between her breasts. She smoothed foundation over her forehead—a second skin barely different from her real skin. Around her eyes, she drew black lines, an almond shape angled at the corners.

"Where are you going?" Colette asked.

"Damn. You made my hand jump." Her mother put the pencil down and wiped the smudge. "Meeting your father at a party."

"Oh." Colette rested her hands in her lap. She stared at them, then looked back at her mother who was brushing color on her eyelids and powdered blush on her broad cheekbones. Colette followed the movement of her mother's hand. She didn't want her to go.

With a deep red pencil, her mother carefully outlined her full lips and then filled in the outline. "Finished," she said as she put the gold lipstick tube down. Turning around, she placed her hands on Colette's shoulders. The child looked sad but she'd be OK with the sitter. "We'll go sledding in the park tomorrow," she said. "Would you like that?"

Colette stared up at the mirror face become three-dimensional. It wasn't a mask because the lips that would kiss her father's cheek at the party were the same lips that kissed her sleepily in the mornings before she went to school. Mother smiled, winked, and no plaster fell away.

In the hall, she stopped to check her hair, one swift pat of the dark chignon as she picked up her coat. "You go to sleep soon," she said. The hem of her slim black dress was crisp; her silver heels click-clicked on the parquet, over the dark wood squares and the pale ones. Her quick hand brushed across the top of Colette's head, ran over the crooked part, pushed the lank hair behind Colette's ears. The lacquered nails fluttered against Colette's cheek. Then she sailed out and the heavy door swung shut.

The sheets will toss against each other under the hard blue sky, then hang still for a moment, smooth as pieces of the best bond paper, before floating up, undulating in the air. The sun will be hot on my cheek when the wind drops, and the smell of mown grass will rise sticky and sweet as raspberry jam. My eyes will skip from one of my mother's bleached sheets to the next, from the dark heart-shaped leaves of the lilac bush to the white clapboard wall, from the deep cloudless sky over the meadow to the red door, behind which the rooms are dim and cool.

Folding a man's underwear, the woman's palms come together and part with a gasp of air. Her hands travel over and over the cloth, hovering and oscillating, dancing like a bee. The thick material droops, rounded in the rear, as she holds up one pair of briefs after another, then lays them flat and smooths the open fly with a few flicks of her fingers. All neatly folded, she piles them next to her own panties edged with stiff lace. The last pair she grabs tightly, dripping from her fist, and brings it to her face. She wipes the white cotton over her red mouth, down and around, round and round her lips, circling her chin with the cloth as she rolls her head, her eyes barely closed so the pale lids flutter.

Colette watches sideways. The woman must feel she's alone, performing some secret ritual, that Colette has disappeared.

In the mirrors lining the walls of the museum shop, Colette's reflections floated gold-toned and flat next to posters, scarves patterned after tapestries, scarabs. From behind the counter, she watched the customers resting books in their bent elbows, heads inclined over the pages covered with fine print and glossy color photographs of paintings, textiles, and pottery. Full, profile, an ear, bits of red mouth—Colette's face gleamed back at her. She felt she was parceled out in the mirrors and each thin self had a different view of the room. Voices bounced off the hard surfaces, rushed together into a white noise.

"Can I see that?" a man asked, pointing to a reproduction of an Egyptian cat. Colette took two of them from the case, rubbing the surface, scratchless, new. When she gave him one, he smiled, looking down at it and at its mate in her fist. "Thanks honey," he said.

The weight of the tiny object pressed her hand toward the glass while the man turned the other one over and over. When he decided he did not want the figurine, she replaced them both reluctantly, for hers had just begun to come alive in her palm.

A woman put a thick book down on the counter. "I'll take this one," she said, draping her red leather gloves over it.

"That will be sixty-six forty-nine, please. A beautiful book, isn't it? The color's perfect, or nearly as perfect as it can be." Colette saw her own lips move along the walls.

As she wrote up the receipt, she smelled Joseph's sheepskin coat behind her. "Colette," he said when she was finished, and she turned, leaned against the counter with her hip.

"I can't talk now. I'm busy."

Joseph watched her fidget with the belt on her skirt like a child he met once, unaccustomed to grown-up clothes. She stared at him as if waiting for him to leave, speak, kiss her, but he knew she'd never say which she wanted.

"I just came to tell you I found an apartment," he said. "Do you want the spider plant or should I take it?"

She opened her mouth and closed it again. Her chin trembled and her tongue was such a soft pink

that Joseph thought for a moment of taking it
between his teeth one more time. Next to her, the
cash register chimed. Paper rustled as the other
clerk wrapped a gift.

"Why didn't you . . . ? What I mean is . . . ,"
she mumbled. "What's the use of talking about
plants? It's time to help this customer now," she
said but didn't turn away, gripped the edge of the
counter until she felt her fingers tremble.

Joseph rubbed his gray hair back and forth so
that it stood up. There'd been a time his rough
hands would play her vertebrae, stop at the top
one beneath her skull. He rubbed the stubble on
his chin, buttoned his coat and then unbuttoned it
again, sliding bone through rawhide loops.

"All right," he said as she put a little girl's
postcards into a bag. "I'll take it." He walked off
through the marble lobby and out the revolving
door to the cold, breathed in the thin rain. As
Colette watched him go, she straightened the soft
bow at her neck, aware that somehow she hadn't
said the right thing.

Knocking the wrinkles out of the patterned
cloth, Colette buttons her blouses and folds them.
When she gets home, she will have to iron them
spread on a towel on the floor. The cats will mew
and crawl over her feet, then take off at a run, leap
from one side of the empty room to the other,
jump to the windowsills and down again, race
across the bed chasing each other. When they've
tired themselves out, they'll lie down near her,
flicking the ends of their tails.

The woman folds shirts that are much too large
to be her own—a blue button-down, a white shirt
with ruffles and French cuffs, a striped one with

each bold stripe a different vibrant color. As if for three different men, Colette thinks. The woman fits the buttons carefully through the holes and lines the side seams up from armpit to hem, smoothing the cloth against the table and tucking the sleeves back against the bodies. There is a certain way of folding a shirt that speaks a meticulousness, a fascination with precision and pleasing, with the stroking of skin as well as cloth, Colette thinks as her hands follow the movements of the woman's hands—slow, steady. She calms her breath.

Turning the knob round in my hand, I'll pull the door toward me, open, and the smell of dry wood will fall out of the red frame and meet the acrid smell of bleach. I'll look over my shoulder again and see the sheets glow and flap gloriously: when they fly and fold over, they'll cast shadows on themselves like indigo birds flitting over the white, and the grass will be a jewel lit from beneath.

Down the hill from the hospital, across the gravel path and passed the neatly clipped yews, Colette chased her father who turned cartwheels against the clouds, twirling into a white no-space. He wore a blue suit and a pale pink shirt that the maid had pressed carefully, starting and ending with the collar. Colette stumbled over the soft uneven earth and the clumps of brown grass, then stopped in the middle of a field where she tipped her head back until her body arched toward the ground, her coat brushing mud, so that she could watch him only.

Following her, the nurses wept into the unseasonably warm air. They complained among themselves that their uniforms had been stained black as if with shoe polish and that their skin had turned the white color of overcooked fish because they had to spend all their time indoors. They whispered:

"Pick her up or she'll fall."

"What a scene, running like that."

"Admonish her."

Colette was dry-eyed, smiling. She enjoyed the multitude of blue star-shapes her father made over the distant trees.

Then the sky emptied. Her mother pushed against the back of her head so that she stood upright and her eyes would overflow. When the fog pried itself loose from the branches at the edge of the field, Colette rose with it or the earth fell away beneath her, a sickening spinning inside. The wind cried cold against her neck, Mother clutched her, holding her to her chest.

Outside, the clouds have rolled in, low and gray; inside the laundromat, a cube of light. Colette takes a sheet from the pile and as she does so, the woman pulls one of her own, a plum-colored one, across the formica toward her. She whips it up so that it flares near the tops of the dryers and then lets it float down. It smells sweet and sheds a violet glow over both of them like a parasol in the sun until it flops around Colette's head and traps her. The bright cotton warm against her hair and shoulders, it presses tightly on the small of her back as the woman reels her in. Colette panics, strikes out, hitting the stretched cloth with her hands, but then can't fight and lets herself be drawn, chambered as in a heart, the reddish air thick around her, while the woman warbles and chortles. She closes her eyes—still the pink light on her lids and the beating bursts of laughter. Then suddenly she's free, disencumbered. The chill air pricks her. When she opens her eyes, the woman is trying to couple the corners of the sheet. "Here," she says, "help me fold this." They dance the rectangle back and forth, pulling it taut, bringing the edges together again.

When they're done, Colette returns to her own sheets which look pale, yellow and dotted with cornflowers. She pays careful attention, shaking one until it starts to fold along clear lines, trying to double it over her arm. The woman comes over and helps her fold the oblong against itself, then her head snaps up and she smiles before turning away. Colette bends down to retrieve a single sock, blue but gray with dust. It isn't hers but she turns it over in her hands for a while.

At the other end of the room, the woman has put her laundry into wicker baskets and is struggling with them while she pulls on the door. Colette hesitates, then hurries to open it for her, standing aside to let the woman out. For a second they face each other, nod before moving apart, and Colette imagines the molecules in their bodies, separate, jostling each other in a silent slanted harmony. The washing machines gleam, distort the reflected light so it's like a coat of new paint, a spill of milk, a long dress of watered silk. Clouds ripple amethyst across the sky.

For a second, I'll stand very still, letting the wind buttress me. The sheets will twist around to touch each other; they'll reflect the sunlight that also strikes the white wall and fills my eyes the way wine fills a glass. Then I'll step through the red door, close it behind me, and walk down the dusty hallway toward the car, listening to the sheets whip and struggle against their pins in a sudden gust of wind.

ASHES

"RED HOT LAVA from the Piton de la Four-
naise volcano cuts through the lush fields of Ré-
union Island at five hundred and fifty feet per
second." We sat under the table, looking at *Na-
tional Geographic,* and I read the captions out
loud to Rebecca. Good strong table, the bolts were
rusty but it was a table we could hide under in an
earthquake. Not that I expected one that night,
but still, we felt safe there. She sat in my lap and
turned the pages, crumpling them. Like blood from
an artery, lava spurted against a dead sky. An
orange stream of lava meandered over the countryside like the tails of an organza bow against green
velvet. When it hit the Indian Ocean, the water
billowed into steam. "Hiss-hiss-hiss," I whispered
in her ear. "A stream of lava one thousand eight
hundred degrees Fahrenheit flows from Mount
Tolbachik," I read. The sky behind that dome was a
hot Day-Glo pink like no sky I'd ever seen anywhere. "Lighthouse of the Mediterranean, the
Stromboli volcano sprays the sky with incandescent ash every twenty minutes." She turned the

page. "None of these look scary, do they?" I said, all the while thinking three thousand curses, nine hundred incantations to keep the one mountain outside at bay.

"No, they're pretty," she said, and we moved on to stories about sharks, New Guinean tattooing practices, struggling irrigation systems in the Sahara. When the doorbell rang, I pushed her away and crawled out to answer it. There were dustballs in the corners.

"It's your Daddy," I called back to her. Behind him, there was the mountain. Sometimes it leaned over the house like a weak old tree in a storm and sometimes the clouds bunched up around it, dark and ominous. In summer, I liked to sit on the stoop and watch the rock climbers dangle at the ends of their ropes—back and forth, back and forth. When one fell I smiled, there would be others. That evening, though, the mountain just sat there. The sun was setting behind the double peak and the sky had a chartreuse glow.

"There's something different about this room," he said, spying around the white walls. Rebecca had paper, crayons, tape, her kindergarten scissors, and the stack of magazines I got for a dime each at the library sale to keep her out of our hair. He took it in oh-so-carefully, trying to see if I'd changed anything yet. Actually it looked exactly the way it did when we first moved there. I couldn't think of any time since when the room had been as neat. The dishes were safely back on the shelves like ladies waiting for tea to be served. So easy to replace after all, though I don't know why I bothered, just had to ask the red-haired clerk at the store to match the fragment and then go home carrying another soup tureen with awful pink flowers painted on the rim.

"Yes. Definitely different," he said again.

I realized that for once I didn't know what in the world he was talking about. I was out of practice. "I know," I said anyway. "There aren't any windows and it's always damp. I'm thinking of putting French doors in along that wall." I wasn't sure he was talking about the darkness or dinginess. There was a hint of sentiment in his eyes. "This is the last time for sentiment," I told him. "This is the last time I'll put up with it."

We both sat on the edges of our seats as if starting a race, and I dumped the deeds, tax forms, health insurance claim forms, snapshots, tuition plan payments for Rebecca's school, loan repayment booklets, and cancelled checks out on the table, spit them up from shoe boxes and paper bags. He tapped his pencil eraser while I emptied box after box—bounce, bounce, bounce, the way he used to bounce Rebecca on his knees. He still did it when he could catch her, but I no longer got any pleasure out of seeing him do it. In the corner by the kitchen door, she started to tape pictures to the walls, photos and diagrams of volcanoes, more and more mountains linked in a jagged mismatched range.

"What is your problem? Why aren't you listening to me?" He didn't whine. He didn't sound in the least peevish. "You're the one who asked me to come over." No, his voice sounded like rocks rolling down a gully. "I'll never understand you," he said, "and I'm not sure I want to. You didn't care one bit about our finances before and now you insist we have to look at all this stuff ourselves. Why can't we be sensible and let the lawyers figure it out? It would be so much easier that way." He sighed and pushed the papers around a little to emphasize what a mess it was, what a mess I was. "It's crazy. We're too tied to it."

I thought about that while he stared at our daughter tacking up Vesuvius. I could only agree that we were crazy.

"And why the hell did you give the kid scissors? She could hurt herself!"

"Jesus! They're safety scissors." It was all I could say. He kept going on about accountants and house payments, rattling off dollar figures, but I just stared at the wall. I wasn't sure any more why I'd invited him and I knew perfectly well what his face looked like. He turned the same ugly red whenever he got mad, and the skin clumped together on his forehead. It was Rebecca I couldn't stop watching. She was still taping those damn volcano pictures to the walls, making a frieze—God knows where she found them all: rivers of molten rock, clouds of steam and smoke, glowing avalanches, black pillow lava, cinders, lapilli, tuff, obelisks of lava traced with orange cracks, ash against the sky like Fourth of July sparklers you hold away from your body afraid they'll burn, technicolor eruptions closing in from all four sides, tightening. She was singing something cheerful and repetitive they taught her at school, "Ring around a rosie," I think. I started to hum along.

"Rebecca, could you be quiet please. Mommy and I are trying to talk." Lump of flesh, he sat back in his chair with his legs spread and elbow on the table. Did the pictures bother him? Or was it her compulsiveness? I waited for him to accuse me of making her compulsive, I knew it was coming. I couldn't deny that I took her out with me in the late afternoon while I waited for the shadow of the mountain to slap us like a giant hand. I was sure it cursed me, it was there every time I opened a door. You'd have thought I'd want to invest in new drapes rather than knock down a wall but I'd planned those windows so we could see the crevices, the boulders balanced precariously, from every room. I wanted to watch the blinking and shuddering, to know what was coming, what was going to happen and when. Yes, I was cursed. Pictures of mountains were always turning up too. Rebecca clicked and hummed in their presence like a Geiger counter, and now, there she was sticking them to the walls. In the pile of junk on the table, there were snapshots someone sent us a few weeks after she was born. In them, lupine and fireweed broke through the ash on a steep hillside and glowed radioactive purple and green. Behind the flowers lay pools of mucky water, naked tree trunks all blown down in the same direction, gray sky. Those pictures drilled their way into me and buried themselves. I imagined ancestors trapped in Pompeii. They'd lived in a villa that lasted out the earthquake. They had frescoes, a mosaic on the floor of a dog just itching to bite someone. Or they'd lived in one of those tall houses on the south side of town near the harbor and painted their walls black to hold down the light. Then they painted white designs on top of that, almost like neon. What did it matter though, all their art and artifacts? They'd gotten it in the end just like everybody else, just like those plums preserved in glass jars. Under the ash their bodies disintegrated, leaving vacuums, and their death agonies were molded in plaster of Paris. Maybe it wasn't agony, I'd never know, but they couldn't have thought they'd be getting up for breakfast the next morning. Sometimes I thought that way too: after a dark night there'd be no resuscitation.

"I don't see why you wanted to do this," he said. He stared at me coldly. I must have been a strange creature that night. Rebecca started another row of pictures above the first, dragging a chair around the room with her. Islands appeared, islands disappeared, mountains opened up like burning hearts.

"We're not getting anywhere," he said.

"Maybe that's what I wanted," I said. It wasn't what I'd planned on saying. I'd planned on being very calm but I couldn't resist. The papers rustled nicely as I shoved them off the table. It was easy to get them all with one sweep of my arm. Rebecca stopped singing, knowing when to retreat. We taught her that if nothing else. I can't say we ever learned the lesson ourselves, though I did know it was sometimes better to sit very still with only my eyes rolling, and that if I had to get away, I should do it as quickly and quietly as possible.

He sighed and didn't look as if he was staring at a stranger anymore but as if it was all too familiar. Well, it was, but I threw my head back and laughed anyway as he bent over to pick up the papers. He was still trying to set things straight, regular as clockwork, tick-tock tick-tock, regular as the Stromboli volcano though not as pretty. How ridiculous he looked, just the way he did when he'd bend over to pick up broken vases, plates and glasses, pots of stew and mashed potatoes, the radio and TV I pushed over one night. Sometimes he'd toss things back at me but he always missed. Just like those other times, his fat ass stuck up in the air. I'd always wanted to kick it but that was one thing I restrained myself from doing. Instead, I'd run through the house with my arms stretched out and scream. When he caught me to keep me from throwing anything else, the fights ended. Or they ended when one of us started to cry and the other rushed to comfort them—at first because we couldn't stand to see the other hurt, then out of guilt, and finally because a crying spouse was simply a nuisance. In any case, the marriage cycled hot then cold like a washing machine.

"I'm going now," he said and didn't even look as if he wanted to slap me; he didn't look at me at all. He kissed Rebecca. "I'll be back to see you soon, honey," he said to her. As I followed him to the front door, I thought I'd leave her pictures up, let her draw over them as much as she wanted, maybe instead of knocking that wall down. Instead of one view, we'd have many—five hundred and fifty thousand volcanoes to remind me where I'd been. Outside, the moon had risen and the snow on the summit glittered sinisterly as if smoke were rising in wisps, nothing to be afraid of yet though it was one of those nights when that bulk of stone seemed even larger than usual, ready to rear up in the yard right across the street. Things could blow at any time. He could come back, we could throw books and sofa cushions, drawing the curtains to protect the windows. We could tip the candles over, watch the conflagration side by side, but he shifted into third just around the bend and I kept myself from crying, knowing that if I started it would be like a rain of ash, silent, very deadly.

ARIADNE IN EXILE

FROM THE SEA, there rise innumerable hilly islands, each densely forested with pines and ringed with palms and juniper bushes. They break through the ocean like scabs, their shores like scrollwork. On some, only a few trees spring slantwise from the rocks; others support villages, a cluster of churches, an airstrip with orange windsock flopping at the end. Around each island, the yellow sand and pink rocks slide down the steep sides of the hills and out under the taut blue-green surface of the water. When the wind shifts to the north and clears the haze from the horizon, waves glint far into the distance toward the main-land where, above a wall of white cliffs, fields spread to the purple mountains, broken only by a grid of dirt roads that lead from one port city to another. Pilots fly from these cities that are never, themselves, visible, bringing washing machines and medicine, record players, newsprint, and presses. They dart down in planes with blue stripes across the tails and leave as quickly. On the islands, people pretend to have forgotten that their own ancestors fought their way from the mainland to these spots of color on the sea; they prefer to believe they've always lived here, that the islands are their past. Ships rarely travel so far anymore although transistor radios pick up country music stations rocking across the water during the still nights in the middle of summer, and when the moon shines, making it seem that city lights are bouncing off the clouds in the east, old men draw the children to them and tell stories about someone who came to live on an island not so very long ago. They sit on the damp grass with children circling them like diamonds around the emerald in a brooch. On the islands, this is all anyone knows of the mainland: distance, technology, stories, a few sounds.

What did the girl do alone on the island?

Summer: she stretched sandaled foot from stone to stone, skirt fluttering above her ankles like the dirty foam that slid off the waves at shore. Poised between steps, she twisted her head, squinted, sniffed at the sea as the wind rode across her skull and spread her hair like a dark stain toward the crumbling styrofoam cups above the high-water mark. She stopped because she saw sails, movement out on the water. No: between the islands, the water was bare, flat as the broad side of a sword. The sun hurt her eyes.

Out the door of her cabin in the morning, she trampled the light into the thick layer of pine needles, then followed the shore to town. Halfway there, she sat between the boulders, scratched hot sand into the soft backs of her knees and let it slide away. The heat prickled, the other islands floated on a shimmer of silver. Like the echo of feet on floorboards, her brother pranced across her mind, making delicate indentations. Every afternoon, Mother would hold the attic door open, hand braced on her hip, chin in the air. She filled the small landing. "Come, come love. Bring that here." Her voice clanked down the stairs while the girl brought the tray from the kitchen, loaded with heavy green dishes, flatware, food. Through the fanlight, sun came and bleached the hall carpet. Outdoors, the farm land dropped suddenly, cleanly, and the sea stretched into the west. She might stop to look out the strip of windows on either side of the front door. "Calm," she might catch herself thinking. But her brother would be hungry, pacing, his hands darting through his hair. At the end of the long second flight, the keys to his room glinted between Mother's fingers like the waves cutting between the rocks at the water's edge. Sun in her eyes, she scanned for those sails and the man manning the tiller. She called him: Theseus, lover, savior, sailor. She rose, her head spinning from the heat.

When she turned from the sea, it was with the knowledge that he'd be standing at the top of the next rise, spread against the trees. She saw him leap like a wall of fire, his arms swinging wide, battling space, to reach her, to lift her. She blinked: gone. Above the green hills, only the white church steeples fingered the blue—the Galilean Gospel Temple, St. Brendan's Episcopal, St. Andrew's Lutheran, St. Mary Star of the Sea. She walked by on Sunday once when the central doors were braced open, and a few people turned white faces to watch her as she stared into a hymn swelling from the dark.

There—the first house with a widow's walk

like a cage on top, flowers the color of blood in all the window boxes. A screen door whistled before it slammed and she jumped, started to walk quickly toward the center of town. The sound of the sea curled over the red and black tile roofs like a wave.

He could be in any of the buildings, watching her from behind a ruffled curtain, waiting to be found if only she weren't so hesitant, knocked on doors, asked questions. She let herself dawdle, scuff the gravel between the gas station and the clothing store where the yellow slickers stood disembodied in the bay window, past the pottery shop where the potter sat outside astride a chair. He called out hello and gave her a new name every day: Elsie, Jane, Prudence, Patience, Hope. It had become a joke they both smiled at after she'd gone by.

In the grocery store she floated past the cashier, holding her skirt gingerly between fingers and thumb. Her hair fell loose from pins, her eyes wide. Softly, slowly, she stopped by the back counter.

"What would you like, dear?" the shopkeeper asked, lifting her chin to see over the case. Her mottled hands slid over the shiny skins of the fish in their trays of ice behind the glass.

"Haddock," the girl said, dragging her voice over the first syllable as she did with the vowels of her own name, then took the cool package wrapped in wax paper and dropped it into her basket.

She walked down to the pier where piles of netting rotted, ropes frayed and stiff with salt. People treated her gently in town, she thought. They understood her loss though she had no memory of

telling them anything. They understood the waiting made her attentive, silent. Perhaps the women
got her story first and repeated it to their men
once she was out of hearing, shaking their heads
all the while. Perhaps he'd talked to the men
before he left, told them to watch out for her. The
boards sagged where she walked. In the harbor
each float bobbed empty of its boat: midday, all at
work far from shore or in the next cove, beyond
the convolutions of the land. She watched the
water come toward her, fought the breeze that
picked up her skirt as if it were trying to dance.

How did the girl come to be alone on the island?
Very simple: she awoke. Through an open door,
she saw a slice of blue and no boat on it, no purple
sail furled around the boom like dead skin. She'd
never seen a sea so empty. At home there were
always white yachts in the harbor and trawlers
out beyond the beakers. And on their zigzag
course from island to island, she'd always woken
with the sail between her and the sky, the man's
breath sliding down her neck—where was he?
She sat up into the dank air. One tiny room. No
windows, just the open door and the sun guided in
along its edge. Across from the bed there was a
rocking chair and next to it, a table. Naked, she
stood in the doorway, careful of the splintered
boards. Under the low green branches of the pines,
the sun scooted up from an inlet that curved into
the hills, the same as on all the islands they'd
seen, shorelines twisted back on themselves like
paths in a maze. To the east the horizon was
blank, as if home had never existed. But she saw
the white cliffs the way they looked from sea—red
in the sunset.

The previous afternoon they had landed at a village dock and walked up a hill, leaning into each other, laughing she remembered, arms linked. They passed the teetering houses and arrived at the square—churches, post office, library, and school placed around a rectangle of green. While he went off to look for food and rope, she sat down near a monument to the war dead with red geraniums planted at its granite base, grass mowed closely around it. The fine hairs were a golden net on his arms as he walked away, and she slumped, curled on her side, and slept. In the morning, she woke to the dark room, triangle of empty water.

Her toes curled on the doorsill. Watery reflections quivered on the tree trunks, but around her, all was quiet, warm, dead. The day she'd opened the door for him the morning glory vines had hung their pink flowers on the air as if on a still lake. He stood in the path looking down at her, his eyes pale opaque blue, the whites as pure as sugar. He smelled clean and cool although the summer dust should have settled on his shoulders. It hadn't rained for months.

"I hear your father wants someone to work in exchange for food and a place to sleep," he said, his voice rich, his vowels flat as the land around them. He hadn't looked as if he needed this job. "They told me all about it in town," he said. "They said he's had trouble keeping people on." Around his head midges spotted the air, and behind them the white buildings on the other side of the bay cast blue shadows against the cliffs.

"Yes, that's right," she said, "to help manage the farm. Mother's lands stretch all the way to there." She pointed to the houses on the outskirts of town. "And there," she said, pointing now to the hills that were only a smudge of violet from where they stood. She thought how she would continue just like this once the estate was her brother's, coming out from the dark house occasionally to stand on the narrow front step and explain the lie of the land to a stranger, looking out over this brightness.

The young man looked away from the fields and up at the house. She had never seen him before, not in town or on any of the neighboring farms; it was not a sailor's face either but something new, blank and beautiful, hiding nothing, his skin absolutely smooth. When he smiled, only one side of his mouth moved and she saw a glimmer as if he knew something he wasn't letting on. It must have been the shadows changing, though, as he turned toward a sound—her brother's laughter rolling from the attic—so familiar she didn't hear it at first, forgetting that someone else might find it strange here—that whooping and hollering—where the fields lay planted with artichokes and cabbages, the farmhands bending over the plants with their short hoes. Smiling to reassure him, she stepped aside and pulled her collar tightly around her throat.

In the parlor the golden hands on the clock, shaped like two pointing fingers, had barely moved since she left the room. Mother turned, tilting her head, and patted the plump sofa cushion for the young man to sit on. By the round mahogany table, Father still dozed with his fingers laced through his beard, his feet planted wide on either side of his chair. She watched the young man, how the pink flushed his cheeks and his eyes floated in the sockets, turning from Father to Mother and back again. He hesitated.

"Sir?" he said and handed over a slip of paper.

Father grunted, but before he could say anything her brother snorted and hissed. She felt the dull creak of the walls and floors under his clumsy weight, the dark storm of sound muffling everything else. Father's eyes were slits of glass.

When the noise stopped, Mother leaned forward so that her pink blouse dipped open, exposing pale skin. "You can go dear." She smiled and nodded encouragingly as if the girl were too young to understand her words. "Go look to him. I'll call you when it's time to show this young man around." There was no doubt that he would be hired. Mother touched him, her hand like knotted wood on his. "Don't mind," she said to him. "You'll get used to it." When the young man looked puzzled, she added, "Our son. He has his own apartments upstairs. He's a bit difficult; we never know when he'll go off like that." She shook her head and the silver earrings rattled. She didn't take her hand off his.

Father was nodding, muttering, trying to conceal his sighs, to disguise his pained expression. "I see you've come about the work," he said finally, waving the slip of paper. "You come highly recommended. You can start right away if you like. It'll be supervising the work in the fields mostly, some other things too. My wife's just bought some more land and it's getting to be a bit too much for me to handle alone." He glanced over at Mother and she nodded absently, staring at the back of the young man's head.

The young man fumbled with his white duck bag. "Thank you, sir. I'm anxious to start."

At the cabin door the trees blocked her view— just a narrow path with the green water pounding the rocks at its end. Where was he? His voice? The burst of expelled air when he held her up over him? She had shown him the dark passage to the barn and the stairs up to the room Mother had assigned to him. Perhaps he went back to town. She bent to see under the branches and fidgeted, her fingers squeezing each other. The sun sprang from the rocks at shore. Her brother didn't like bright light. The one time she'd brought a lantern with her, he'd jumped up, arms wider than she was tall. His screams had sliced the air, his feet a shiny black whir as he pawed the floor. Her heart beat in her throat, hands stiff and useless until she thought to blow out the flame. After, she'd always tended him at dawn or in the dusty, murky noontime haze. She'd had all the attic windows boarded up.

She turned back inside. At the table she slipped her dress over her head; it still smelled of salt. He'd left all her clothes. Why? Her sandals, other dress, warm cloak for winter—the one they'd wrapped themselves in that first night on the water before they'd managed to break into the cubby and pull free two rough blankets. He'd left a sack of groceries, a plastic jug of water, money. She counted it, bills so soft they could be made of cloth, so much money he must mean to be gone a long time. She folded it smaller and smaller until it was just a dense square of paper.

Beneath her the bed was hard, but he'd provided sheets, a thin pillow, several woolen blankets folded at the foot. Perhaps he planned on being back after the first leaves had fallen. Still, that was months and months away. Why? Through the door the sun fell straight. She flung her arm across her eyes and slid down close to the wall. Hard

hands, pink cheeks, tan feet branded by the straps
of his sandals, hair like chains, thighs that held
hers like irons—she'd wish him back, wish back
the curl of his lip, the tendons distended in his hand
as he held the sails through a storm, knuckles
white as the waves kicked up around the boat.
He'd taken her away from the farmhouse with its
long hallways and twisting stairs and out onto the
sea. Deceptive: from her window at home, the
water had always been the tight silver surface of a
plate, not a puzzle of currents and undertow. After
tacking between the islands he'd finally brought
her here: one dark room and the tortuous coastline outside the door. Why? She pulled her legs up
close to her body. He'd said little about his past,
nothing about where they were going. She hadn't
cared. He'd held rakes like spears, dinner plates
like shields. Suddenly he'd opened his arms, asked
her to go.

For months she'd lain awake waiting for her
alarm clock to ring and wondering if he were
already up at the other end of the house, pulling
on his pants, rubbing his wet face with a towel. As
he carried the garbage away from the attic, she
watched the lamplight disappear from his back,
then climbed, grabbing the dusty rail, to make up
her brother's bed and groom him with the silver
comb Mother had provided in its own suede
pouch. As she fought the snarls, she thought of
these new possibilities—that there were people in
the world she'd never met, places she'd never
been. She thought of the jet trails the young man
had pointed out to her, far above the house.

At night they met again. Her back against the
wall, she couldn't swallow, took quick shallow
breaths until he had walked down the hallway

toward his room. She could turn then, let a rat
loose in her brother's apartments as she did every
night, stamping so it would run the tunnel of passages to the bedroom. In the morning, there was
always a spattering of blood around her brother's
mouth to clean; it was dry, brown, and he let her
pull it free with her fingernails, grumbling a little.

Silence reminded her where she was. The birds
had stopped singing. Under the sheet it seemed
grayer, as if the sky had clouded over or the sun
moved behind the house. A rough weave, the
cloth let in thorns of light. Had she not been
pretty enough for him, full-fleshed? But in the
boat he'd often called her his beauty. Had she not
responded quickly to his touch? Did she sing too
much during the day? Or had she failed to chant
him to sleep? She'd never complained that she
could remember, but perhaps she'd been found
wanting in fortitude. Perhaps she'd recited a poem
more than once, boring him.

His shirt stretched tightly across his chest.
Every afternoon her father had gone to find him
outside. She saw them standing just where the dry
grass gave way to the green irrigated rows of vegetables. Both men bent their heads as they talked,
their caps tipped low over their eyes, and the
younger man always tapped the ground with a
stick as if considering what the other had to
say but unsure whether he agreed. If he saw her
watching from behind the stiff parlor curtains, he
gave her a half-smile and then turned so she could
not see his lips move. Father gestured toward the
house, speaking fervently, pointing in turn to the
servants' wing, the dark green shades of Mother's
boudoir, her own bedroom, and then up to the
roof.

Later, she leaned on the dining room table with the heels of her hands and looked out the window behind the young man's blond head. "I can't leave my brother," she said. "You know that. No one else can care for him." She thought of her brother listening for her step as though the chores were done automatically by a body, her body, which somehow could not be replaced. She saw herself going upstairs, charmed, unable to stop, and all her feelings left on the landing.

He reached over the table toward her. "Let's go tonight," he said again, pleading, nervous. "Let them fight it out themselves. It'll be better that way, you'll see."

"What do you mean, fight it out? "

"Just come with me. If you want to come back, you'll be able to, later."

"I can't," she whispered until her refusal was the song of all their meetings, the silent refrain while they sat at supper with her parents and talked about the crops, weather, politics in town. "I can't say why," she said later, the china bowl she held stained magenta from the beets they'd eaten. "I'd feel too guilty. He'd be alone."

Outside, the young man worked, the sky spread about like a quilt.

"Give me a little more time," she'd said. Inside, something gnawed at her—to climb a mountain and breathe the thin air at its peak, to step into a boat and sail to the edge of the world—but she couldn't agree.

"Time won't change anything," he mumbled, and a fine network of lines formed on his forehead. "We can't wait any longer." He grunted as he struck the spade into the earth, wouldn't turn around again even after she'd reached the house. He didn't speak to her for days, and she'd found him closeted more often with her father, found them whispering in the hayloft, the grainfield, and in the corner behind the stairs.

Unable to dissuade him, she'd stood on the landing, her lantern sending a thread of light after him through the partially open door. He'd broken her down; he'd been relentless. "It's too late for me to spare you now so you might as well help me. At least show me the way." How hard had she tried in the end? She couldn't even grab his arm to hold him back. Her brother—splashing and clawing as she bathed him, willing to eat only after he'd tossed his food to the floor and made her scoop it up again—was harder to control than this young man would have been. She could have stopped him with one word, said yes. Instead, she stood in the dark, the house silent, and thought how this year, all ties broken, her days would lighten, have a slow rhythm all their own. She would not have to lead her brother downstairs on his birthday, clean and combed. She would not have to watch him drink whiskey with the girls from town while they sat on his lap, fed him cake and ice cream, braided the hair on his massive chest and left the pink marks of their lipstick in it. They tickled his ears with straw until he, playfully, swatted at them, tossed one over his shoulder and carried her upstairs, the others following. For the rest of the evening, Father sat in a corner with a glass and a decanter of brandy, and she sat on the arm of his chair with her sweater wrapped tightly around her, afraid of any noise, waiting to see if all the girls came down again near dawn and how much money her mother slipped into their palms. She would not have to care for him at all; someone else would do it.

The young man had disappeared. He'd begged her, pleaded. Once, tears had even come to his eyes which he wiped away with his fingers. Still, she'd perversely said no. Now she followed him in her mind, heard the slab of oak rasp the floor, felt the rough wooden attic walls as he slid his hand along them, making his way toward the bedroom where a few rays of moonlight came through the shutters. She followed, all his blond hair gone black; together they anticipated the narrow opening where the darkness grayed a little. Her brother would be sleeping on his straw in the corner, but at the sound of feet approaching he would wake, stand on hairy legs, tilt his head around the doorway, and sniff with his flat nose to discover who was coming.

The time she had, so unwisely, brought a lamp at night, she'd found him like that—neck craned, watching, a savage look in his eyes. Once she'd put the lantern down, the shadow of his square head and shoulders slanted up the walls and ceiling. He'd leapt, ears twitching, crushed her to him and ripped her dress. He'd bent to lick her face, neck, breasts with his thick tongue as if to lick all the salt off her. He held her tighter, scratched his stiff white hair into the slime he'd left. Rubbing his body against hers, he spread his hand between her thighs. His sharp hooves trod her feet. When she screamed, he only snorted and blew damp breath, clutching her tighter still. Finally, her father had freed her with his whip, yanked her from the attic and, hushing her so she wouldn't disturb her mother, brought her down to the black quiet of her room where he left her, warning her never to say anything about the episode.

She shivered, remembering, but part of her entertained the thought that things might change now. The land could be hers, not her brother's. She'd tear down this house and build a new one—spacious rooms, no halls, immense windows—but the vision was shattered by a volley of curses from the hall behind the almost closed door, screeching, echoing. She shook, and the patterned wallpaper flickered as she swung the lantern. She had imagined a silent meeting, not this which would surely wake the house and bring her mother stumbling up the stairs. She had seen the young man stare her brother down, subduing him with those bright eyes and thought then—what? She didn't know. There'd been a blank space. The screams grew louder, nearer, and a hollow thump-thump-thump followed them. She sent a sliver of yellow light through the door, calling to the man, listening to him run lightly toward her and to her brother trot unevenly, slowly, wheezing deeply, fall. The man burst through the door and slammed it behind him.

She never asked how the pursuit had ended, stood frozen in surprise as the silence gathered again. He'd stumbled through the door and swept her down the stairs—the first time he'd touched her, hot steel. He'd stepped through the door, stripped off his drenched shirt, and pressed her to his smooth chest, his cold skin. Awkwardly, she'd held the lantern aside. Not a scratch on him but his white shirt was red with blood. What weapon had he taken? In the yellow light his eyes shone purple, but by the time he helped her into the boat they were the same calm blue as always.

And he'd taken her away, quick note left on the sideboard, dark sail under the moon. Although the night was warm she shivered beneath her cloak, numb, looked back and saw lights come on in the house, awake, a vigil. She imagined her mother's hysterics, pounding the floor with her fists, Father comforting her roughly.

"You are glad you came with me, aren't you?"

She dipped her hand into the water without answering.

"You wouldn't want to be back there now. There's everything in front of us, the whole world."

He'd thrown off his shirt in a wide, grand motion, and left it on the stairs. His chest had tasted salty.

"I wanted to come," she said at last and went to sit next to him. "Of course I did. There was never any question about that."

Until the points of light on shore were no larger or brighter than stars, everything was silent.

"I've never killed anyone . . . ," he started, rubbing his palms together. She reached out and stuck her hand between his to silence him.

They spent their nights in the bottom of the boat, swells pressing against the hull, one swell and then another until she wasn't sure whether the rocking was the sea's movement or their own wild tumbling in that sharp space. The halyard tink-tink-tinked against the mast. She slept most of the day too, curled in the sun, and when she woke up, reached for him. His fingers were a drug of forgetfulness; she thought they were crossing Lethe.

How did the girl spend her time on the island?

Winter: she went into town less frequently, following the road when she did, a strip of white on white. The houses lay back in the landscape, sucked up by snow. Around them the pines were black, the palms dauntlessly green. Out over the water the fog twisted around the islands like scarves around a throat.

At home she arranged and rearranged her few belongings, lining up jars on the shelf, folding blankets into squares of the same size, opening and refolding them more precisely. She sat by the table and knit, leaving the door open to smell the snow because the snow smelled of salt. She positioned her chair so that, when she looked up, she could see through the falling snow to the water, waiting for a flash of purple. She looked up often; jittery, she couldn't sit still. When she felt the cold on her ankles, she swept the snow out the door and closed it, then pulled her chair closer to the stove where the water boiled for the tea she drank constantly. The liquid warmed her. Cold comfort her mother taught her to knit—the thin tough hands had held her own around the needles, clumsy stiff movements. Her mother's hands fought to keep her fingers moving correctly. Together they made wide ribbons for her brother who tied the colors around his head. When one of her hairs fell free, she wrapped it with her needles, knotted herself in. The material dropped to the floor, spread under the table, chair, bed, the color of the winter sea, gray-green. She had an idea that if she knit a net fine enough and wide enough, she could cast it over the waves, entangle him and draw him back. Through the winter she worked on it. Once before she had pulled him free, blond hair shining suddenly, from the dark, but then, of course, he'd wanted to come. In the spring, she thought, she'd stand on the promontory, fling her net out and reel him in, the pattern of her fabric embossed into his clean, red, salty skin. He'd turn and turn in the waves, his body rising in the swell, and the water would shine around the dark form she could see from shore. She floated, her breath lifting her body.

He might be lost at sea and pining for her. In which case, once he found his way back to the island, they would make the cabin their home, cut windows in the walls to let in the light, order pots and pans from a catalog and bed sheets in bright colors. She smiled, saw him tapping his fingers impatiently against the gunwale.

He might be dead, a skeleton, a web of bones in the stern of the boat. A tremor started in her stomach and spread; she couldn't stop shaking. The stench of his rotting flesh was everywhere. Still, at least she'd know, sail up or down, mast gone, anchor ripped loose or pulled into the boat. She'd know how he died: thin bone-hands pressed under his cheek as he slept, the shape of a child.

He could be eight hundred miles away in her sister's arms saying, "Poor girl. I miss her so. I cried for days when she disappeared overboard." He licked her sister's neck and she tweaked his earlobes with dainty baby hands. Such treachery! The image slid across her knitting, but she didn't know where it came from as she didn't have a sister. She stared at their body parts magnified, distorted by the rippling cloth, twining and relaxing. Her fingers slowed, she enjoyed the sour taste, the stiffness of her mouth. She didn't care; she would get him back, she could do anything. Rising, she tossed her knitting to the floor and strode the length of the cabin—stove to door, table to bed. When she looked outside, the storm was a blur of white. She let the fire burn out.

Once, in a gale, the potter came from town to make sure she had wood and food to last out the storm and found the cabin door propped open. He stood thinking how he should have come sooner, until the sound came up from the inlet on the wind, and he saw her on the ledge howling—the only name for that noise—with her arms thrust behind her and her skirt plastered to her thighs. When he took her hand, she came quietly but as if she didn't know what was happening to her.

The weather cleared and she wandered into town, her mass of tangled hair tucked under a black knit cap. At the pottery shop the precise semicircles of earthenware and porcelain in the windows drew her inside. She studied bowls and cups like a bride intent on choosing a pattern, picked up vases and platters to follow the scenes painted on them, the bright glazes smooth against her palms. When the floor sounded under her heavy boots, the potter opened the curtains at the back of the room and stepped through. He beckoned to her, a short dark man, beard straggling across his face. "Come," he said, putting a gray, clayey hand on her arm. "It's warm in the back."

As he looked at her, she thought to say, "No. Leave me by the light. I'm waiting for someone." It wouldn't have been a lie, but she followed him into the other room where he took her bulky winter coat and pressed her into the corner of a couch, its chintz greasy and faded.

"I'll show you my new ones," he said and brought them from the cluttered shelves. "My animal plates."

She was aware of his gaze, how he hovered
behind the couch and then in front of it, aware of
how his forehead furrowed and unfurrowed in
complex and changing patterns as she tried to feel
the line where one color became the next, fore-
ground became background, where on one plate
the white bull's horns lay bonded to the green.

"You like them," he said. "I can tell."

The animals were caught behind the glassy surface, staring past her blankly. They scared her; she
could not say whether she liked that feeling or
not. "They remind me of things. Is that why you
made them? Do they remind you of things too?"

"I don't think so," he said. "I just made them,
that's all. I don't remember much." He sat down,
squeezing between her and the corner of the
couch, his thigh surprisingly hot, put his hand on
her knee. He was whispering so that she had to
lean very very close to hear.

What did the girl think of her past?

Through the fall and winter she thought that
she had been saved and then abandoned; she
didn't know why. She thought her father, the
king, was the son of a girl kidnapped and raped by
a god in the form of a bull; her mother was the
daughter of the sun and moon; her brother, with
his thick tongue, the frenzied eyes of a man in
pain, the wispy hairs at the end of his tail, was the
fruit of their mother's monstrous passions. She
believed she would be delivered again, soon. As
the snow continued to pile up beneath the trees,
her taste for isolation wore thin and she wanted to
go back to the knife-slice coast of the mainland,
the turrets of her childhood home. She refused to
let herself think how not even the charm of roy-

alty had saved her family from the meanderings of the heart.

Once, when she was four, she saw her mother ravaged by a bull after climbing inside the wooden cow a carpenter had fashioned for her. He finished the beast, sanding the rump smooth, while she sat under the table and Mother paced impatiently between the work bench and the window, clutching the front of her dress and stirring the sawdust with her toes. Outside, the bull trotted, white against the green east meadow, and then stopped, chewing, his jaw sliding sideways, tufts of hair springing from the ears behind the curved horns. When the real animal mounted the wooden one in the courtyard, she ran toward them, screeching. The pine creaked and groaned, and the carpenter swept her up before she even reached the open air, closing the door, covering her eyes and mouth, pressing her to his leather apron so that her body was bruised by the screwdrivers and chisels lined up in the pockets across his chest.

In the spring when she paced the narrow porch of her cabin, breaking the new forsythia twigs between her fingers, she recalled that all her years at home had been an imprisonment. The promise began outdoors where the straight rows of vegetables replaced the dark passageways and led to the sea. She felt her father's dread, heard her mother's imperious voice. She recalled how the house lights switched on as soon as they'd pulled away from shore as if someone had been waiting for her to leave, as if her father had woken her mother with one hand while he reached for the light cord with the other. She left because she thought her hand was forced, but that was no reason to return. She left because her young man had

threatened and cajoled, because she had forced
him into taking her away or, what amounted to
the same thing, did not stop him from unlocking
the heavy oak door to the attic, believing then that
he was her only egress from fear and the pleasure
she found in it.

Did the girl ever leave the island?
No. Under a worn brown blanket the potter's
mattress held the indentations of their bodies like
a cup. His little arms and legs sidled up against
her. In summer they threw off the sheets. His kiss
was different each time: violent, passionate, delicate, dry. She fought back, laughing, and they
slept as if a saber lay between them.

He shaped dishes for her. Around the circum-
ference of a plate, in the well of a bowl, she told
the stories she'd only told herself before, re-
imagined now with black figures on red, red figures on black.

Theseus had shrunken, muscles like unraveling
rope, hair thinning. He had drifted for over a year
without a chart, under a reddened sky, unable to
read the stars. All around the islands the sea had
been flat and shiny as a ball gown's blue silk; the
fishing boats on it, far and white. When she pulled
him ashore, he was so weak that she had to carry
him up the slope beneath the palm fronds and
pines, his arms dangling to the ground, and he
looked up at her in fear, as if she might be the
angel of death. She flipped him into the air, tossing him, catching him, as she walked barefoot
over the sharp stones.

In the morning all was silent. Her head ached,
a dull throb like a memory: her brother, alone,
crawled a complex of passages, visiting various

rooms that all looked the same, one image of collapse after another; outside in the dark hall her parents passed without looking at each other, her father stroking his beard, Mother shriveling inside her black dress; then she saw them seated together at the dining room table, her brother in a black bow tie, using a knife and fork, all lifting glasses, clinking crystal loudly, drinking. Shadows, they stained her body, and she realized they'd taunt her always. She raked her fingers through her hair, lashed out, rolled her eyes, bellowed, had trouble telling one of her limbs from another until the man moved beside her, broke through with noise.

JUNE 4, 1469

WE ARE IN FLORENCE in the dark after
midnight. The river shushes like curtains: opening and closing over the Arno. Up ahead, Giuliano
rides with my father while I sit and rock in the
carriage with Mother and Clarice, listening to the
horses' hooves strike the stones. Tomorrow my
sister, Clarice, will marry Giuliano's brother, Lorenzo. I've opened the window a bit for some air
although Mother shakes her head, no Lucrezia; the
night is hot and damp, and the walls pass close to
the side of the carriage, water trickling over the
blocks and glimmering in the light from our
torches. From the hill I tried to see the cupola of the
duomo—the largest in Christendom—but the
night is too black.

Clarice is nodding; I'm sure she's dreaming of
Lorenzo, dreaming of sitting next to him in church
and glancing at his profile as she did once last year,
secretly, sideways, across all of St. Peter's. She
must have turned slightly and glimpsed his dark
head above everyone else's, his great collar of white
lace falling over his chest as he leaned forward,

hands on knees, listening carefully to the choir just as she hoped he would be. How can she sleep when we're in Florence and tomorrow she's marrying a man who writes sonnets, a patron of the arts whose tutor was Ficino, the translator of Plato? The Medici, like my husband's family, are only too happy to marry their son to a daughter of Giacopo Orsini.

In Clarice's dream, her sister, Lucrezia, is a red shape swinging through a doorway into the bedroom, her skirts suspended like a bell. Father walks toward Clarice along the hallway, smiling and holding out his hand, his cane tapping the marble. Behind him, candles flicker. They topple from their holders, fall to the floor, and burn for a while—he doesn't come any closer—then go out. For a minute, Clarice still sees the golden medallions of candlelight shaking before her. She is left standing in the dark; the air is fragrant with wax.

One of Clarice's hands lies in her lap. The fingers twitch the way a dog's leg does in its sleep. Mother holds Clarice's other hand carefully, protectively, between her own. As we rattle over the cobbles, she smiles at me, the lines sinking deeper on either side of her mouth. We wind through the streets to the Palazzo Alessandri where we will spend the night.

In Rome my husband is asleep in the palace his family has lived in for centuries. Sometimes I bring in chunks of stone that have fallen from the cornice to the street to show him how sorely the building is in need of repair. I carry them close and heavy in both arms like an eight-month baby, but my husband waves me from the room, saying he has better use for his money than to spend it on decorations. I've often thought how I'd like to drop a stone, turn

and leave it, ringed with mortar dust on the carpet,
but I always carry them with me when I go.

Giuliano opens the carriage door and the torches
glow orange on the palazzo walls. By the gate a
servant stands, shielding a candelabra from the
breeze with her heavy arm. I touch Clarice's thigh
to wake her and step down, stand weak-kneed on
the uneven stones just behind Giuliano's broad
back, his tunic stretched tight across it. I let my
shawl droop from my hot shoulders. Mother extends her long fingers, her slender wrist, and her
foot from the carriage into the glare, and shadows
play over them, a brocade. Father takes hold of her
hand, lifting it with one of his own as a gentleman
should and places his other hand beneath her foot
so that she can pause there, leaving the imprint of
her heel in his palm before stepping to the ground.
The servant curtsies, dipping her plump chin to
her breast, and the housekeeper steps out of the
dark with her gray hair flitting like bats' shadows
around her head. She, too, lifts her skirts, exposing narrow ankles and well-worn shoes. Hooves
echoing, Giuliano's horse trots off, carrying him
home. We are hurried upstairs—our hosts already
asleep—with the housekeeper's candles ahead of
us and the servant's tapers behind tossing us wavering on to the walls; Clarice's head is bowed and
her graceful hand strays to her throat, fingering the
small gold cross.
My room is large, dark. Clarice shares my bed as
she used to when we were children. She would
sprawl, belly down, with her arms and legs thrown
over me, breathe deeply, sigh in her sleep. Tonight
she lies straight-backed. At the windows the curtains float up on the warm breeze that spills the

sour smell of the river like wet ink across the floor to the bed, dampening the sheets. My sister has her hands crossed on her breast.

"Clarice," I whisper, "are you awake?" I touch her elbow.

"Yes, Lucrezia."

After she is married, Clarice will have a new sister named Lucrezia—Lorenzo's sister, called simply Crezia. She has heard that the new one laughs all the time. The day after her wedding this woman laughed for so long that the servants were ordered to pour buckets of cold water over her head so that she could stop and catch her breath. Clarice's real sister Lucrezia laughed also, but before she was married; the little gurgles chased one about the house, always disturbing the quiet.

"I didn't think you'd be able to sleep. With all the preparations, you've never told me Clarice, but aren't you excited? Living in Florence. . . . In the evenings, Lorenzo will read sonnets to you. He'll play Petrarch to your Laura, Dante to your Beatrice. He'll settle his arm around your waist, hold the candles high, and show you the rooms, each painted by a different artist." She looks at the ceiling for a bit before turning to me. "Do you think he's handsome, Clarice? As handsome as Giuliano?" Mother has already told me that Lorenzo is almost ugly, with a swarthy complexion, a flat nose, and a high-pitched voice. She warned me to say nothing to Clarice who wants to have beautiful children. If I were marrying Lorenzo de Medici, I wouldn't care about physical beauty.

Clarice dreamed that Father was approaching and there was the dark, smoky smell of wax. He stuttered and screeched, "Ri-ri-ri-ricci," calling her pet name. Then, in her dream, the rocking motion of the carriage threw her to her knees, bruising them, and once again she saw Lorenzo across the church aisle. In looking away from her father's wrinkled neck, she took her thoughts off her prayers and was unable to return to them no matter how hard she tried to remember the words. She stared at Lorenzo's dark head, her eyes carved open.

Warm breeze washing over her, Clarice wonders if Florence always smells as rotten as this. She decides she will never leave the windows open; the damp makes her bones hurt.

"Remember, Lucrezia, that this match is good for our family. It joins two of the most important families of Italy just as your marriage joined two of the oldest families in Rome. Now hush, we should sleep. See how the sky is already turning gray."

Clarice closes her eyes and the lids are smooth and white, rounded like opals set into the marble of her skin. I almost tap them to feel their coolness but turn on my side instead and try to sleep.

The curtains move. Not long ago, Clarice was with Mother on retreat. She visited one of the Sisters at night; the nun's cell was small, cold, dark, and she slept on a narrow bed with a thin straw mattress and one brown blanket thrown across it.

"Highly irregular, Miss," the nun said, but then she sat down again and let Clarice hold her hand. Clarice could not understand how it was warm and soft in that room, expecting to grasp something cold, wrinkled, rough. The Sister let Clarice describe how she had sinned in a dream and then sent her back to bed. In the dream, someone had chiseled away her flesh and she gloried in the lightness and elegance of her newly exposed

bones. As she spoke, delicate shivers ran up and down her back.

The sky is pale blue and the sun barely reaches over the houses across the street, but the day is already warm, the air still and heavy. While Mother helps Clarice dress, I sit by the open window and look out at the horses below. The humidity hangs, suspended like a veil on the heat. Clarice sits on a stool with her back perfectly straight as she always sits when her hair is being brushed. Even the day we both had our ears pierced, she sat perfectly calm. Briefly she pouted, but Father shook his finger, told her to be brave, and she let them drive the golden posts through her earlobes. When my turn came, I dodged tables and maids until they called the footmen in from the pantry to catch me and hold me down.

Bending over, Mother quickly fastens each of the fifty hooks up the back of Clarice's gold brocade dress, and her long braid falls over her shoulder, a dark stripe against her gray sleeve. Mother breathes heavily for she's gotten stout.

"Come here Lucrezia, and fix your sister's hair," Mother says as she fastens the last hook. She drapes the emeralds around Clarice's thin neck which Lorenzo's Mother has praised, and I walk toward them with the morning sun warm on my back.

I grab Clarice's reddish hair. It hangs below the seat of her stool and there's so much of it I can't hold it all in both my hands. Separating it into strands and then weaving them together with white and gold ribbons, I watch my wedding band disappear in the plaits and appear again, another glint of gold.

"Hold your head up or this will be uneven," I say

and pull the hair tighter, the skin taut across her temples. Clarice lifts her head and lets us see her face.

"You're so pale dear," Mother says. Clarice isn't smiling. Her lips are the color of carnations.

Taking her soft skin between thumb and forefinger, gently I pinch her cheeks and slap them lightly with my palms. "You're beautiful, so beautiful," I say. "Shy. Like a feather," but she doesn't smile. "Lorenzo will be writing innumerable poems about you," I say. "Poems about your eyes." Clarice's eyes, the color of dark honey, look slowly up at me. "About all your copper hair, how it drops heavily when you undo the braids."

Clarice knows that Mohammedan women are always veiled, swathed in black, and she thinks that she would like to be able to pass a mirror and glance into it and not have to see herself but a mass of cloth instead. With his quivering, spotted hands, her father strokes the air near her hair sometimes as if he is stroking a veil. His brown lips mumble, you are rich, you are rich. This past half year, she has often felt she should thank him for this marriage, because it meant she could do something for him, but the thought of the great distance between Florence and Rome made her tremble so with fear and excitement that she could only take his dry, old, mothlike hand from her hair and pat it.

In her lap, Clarice's hands clench into fists as if she's squeezing a small animal. She doesn't seem to hear me or even to see me, but she says, "Lucrezia, please be sensible." I lean closer to her ear. "About your lovely bosom." Clarice doesn't blush. "About the soft hairs on your thighs."

On the other side of the room, Mother is chuck-

ling. She has her arms crossed over her breasts.
"Come now, Lucrezia. It's time for you to dress,"
she says, still laughing.

"I am sure Lorenzo writes fine poetry," Clarice
says. "He can write as easily about your hair as
about mine."

I step aside and the sun streams through the
window, carried on the fine, floating particles of
dust and mist, and spills, sparkling, over Clarice
who sits so calmly in her gold dress with her hands
neatly laid in her lap. She is heavenly light; she is
untouchable.

Downstairs, Clarice mounts a white war horse, a
present to Lorenzo from Ferrante, King of Naples.
Moisture collects on the horse's soft nose, then
drips to the cobbles in a spattering of dark drops.
When he lifts his head and shakes his braided
mane, rolling back his yellow eyes, bells tinkle and
their silver reflects the sun, sending spots flying
over the fine houses lining the narrow street. The
humidity slides over my skin warm as silk that's
been out in the sun. As I reach to pat her knee, my
sister grants me one of her smiles that always seem
like a gift, and I take my place in the procession
behind Mother's gray train. Father leans on her
arm, nodding his bald head and grinning as she
speaks. Behind us, the noble families of Florence
have assembled.

*The groom pulls Clarice's horse along, and the
procession starts across the city to the Palazzo
Medici. Perhaps, as that building is newer, Clarice
thinks, it will be less dusty and I will not sneeze
so much. It is newer even than the annex in the
back of the house in Rome where Giacopo Orsini
has his study and keeps his pigeons. On the way*

home from church, Clarice often passes the damp,
earthy place where, after all these years, they have
not yet paved the new courtyard. As she looks up
at her father's closed windows, she tries to keep
the smell from making her sick.

Following the horse's slow pace, we turn along
with the street, the musicians up ahead drumming
our progress. In my blue satin and pearls, I'm
already hot. The crowds have come out; people in
ragged clothes hold their children back. Women
push loose hairs out of their faces with filthy
hands, and men lean in the doorways, cross their
legs, laugh. They are always spitting and swear-
ing. Our route should have been more carefully
planned.

Clarice sways up ahead on her horse, and I can
see her white neck between her gold dress and her
copper hair. She must be thinking of Lorenzo waiting for her in his fine suit edged with silver piping,
be trembling at the thought of how he'll press her
hands between his own, fingers together as if in
prayer, how she'll suddenly feel how warm his skin
is. I'd just want him to take my arm and lead
me through the streets of Florence, through the
cloisters and churches and the council chambers of
the town hall, to show me paintings and sculpture,
to discuss Virgil and Aristotle, his voice low and
clear and light in my ear all the while.

I hold the folds of satin up with my hands and
step carefully over the cracks in the paving stones.
Over us the sky is a soft stretch of blue between the
buildings. In Rome my husband is most certainly
still asleep with his white nightshirt tangled
around his fat legs, his arm thrown straight across
the bed, and his mouth wide open. Little Caterina
is being fed by her nurse. The woman has a perma-

nent collar of grit, and one can easily hear that she comes from the south. While she feeds my daughter her eggs, she'll sing those silly rhyming songs the farm children sing down there, and she'll scratch her head over the food.

We pass Orsanmichele where a saint occupies each niche; they watch us as we go with blank stone eyes and smile at my sister's beauty. St. George carries the crest of Florence on his shield; he twists in his niche and stares from under a furrowed brow. His dragon is still ahead of him, the Milanese threat, the tyranny of the Visconti. He is young, but he could reach forward and fell any intruder with his sword. Even I, with my sheltered upbringing in Rome, know something about this city's history. I listened at the right doors and heard my father grumbling about the republic of Florence. I heard his friends talking about Ghiberti's bronze doors on which each scene from the life of Christ fits perfectly into its quatrefoil panel. Although the doors were then already forty years old, the old men spoke of them as if they were news.

The white horse walks steadily, ploddingly. How could he be meant for war! Last night, Lucrezia's wedding raced through Clarice's sleep, all four days of feasting. There were irises everywhere and the guests sat among the flowers eating variously cooked and stuffed birds—capons, geese, ducks. They chewed noisily on the bones, and Lucrezia had a circle of grease the color of amber around her red and swollen lips. Clarice cracked the bones open on the table and sucked out the marrow; the sound was louder than music and she had never tasted anything so sweet.

Now, we pass the duomo where the evangelists sit and the baptistery with its great doors swung open. The crowds are thicker here; their brown and gray clothes fill the wide plaza under the hazy blue sky, under the doves that flap and dive in circles around the dome. The bells are ringing in Giotto's campanile. The whole city has come out to see my sister, but she stares at the braided mane of her horse while I gaze around in wonder at the rippling line of people, meeting their eyes.

One more block up the Via Larga is the Palazzo Medici. Giuliano steps out of the crowd and he and my father lift Clarice down from her horse, straighten her gown behind her. Clarice grabs me and smiles and squeezes my hand warmly.

"Don't look so startled," she says in her child's voice. I remember she is seventeen. "I am only getting married." She kisses me softly, slowly on the cheek, lingering. Then Giuliano leads her off through the loggia into the courtyard. As the crowd parts for them, an olive branch is hoisted. She leans toward him like the sails of a boat in the wind.

In the center of the courtyard, a bronze statue of David with the head of Goliath stands on a pedestal, and all around it servants scurry to prepare the tables. The air is filled with the sharp sound of their snapping the damask cloths up and the silence as they let the thick material balloon down over the boards. Lorenzo waits in the chapel. Leading Clarice by the hand, Giuliano shows us the first stairway on the right where he gives her to Father and steps aside, motioning for us to climb the dark stairs first. This is what she will remember—the yellow sunlight falling over the David in the courtyard, Lorenzo waiting, her family following her up the stairs and our shoes scuffing the stones behind her.

In the chapel, Lorenzo rearranges his lace cuffs and brushes dust from his black velvet coat as we are seated in delicate gilt chairs and provided with stools for our tired feet. He watches my sister approach, walking toward him still staring at the ground, at the carpet of petals that has been spread for her. Mother was right: he is not beautiful. With his square chin lifted and his mass of coarse black hair, he looks proud, willful, dispassionate. His eyes travel quickly from one of us to the next, picking up some detail to understand us by. When Clarice reaches the altar, she glances at Lorenzo and longer at Giuliano who stands beside him. He has been kind and attentive; Lorenzo is still unknown, but he is beginning to smile as if he is amused by Clarice's head weighed down by her ribbons and braids. The priest intones the marriage canon.

Lorenzo's skin is the same color as the meat of roasted chestnuts. He smells of horse. Or perhaps it is Clarice from the ride across the city. That is as it should be, she thinks. Our perfumes are all vanity. When Clarice was very little, her father gave her a present of a bird—some gaudy thing that died the first cold day in autumn. She took it to the courtyard early in the morning and burned its iridescent feathers one by one. When the cook came out and asked Clarice what she was doing, she hid the naked bird in her apron and said she was burning love letters.

I turn to the willowy figures in the fresco of the Adoration of the Magi that circles the chapel. On

the walls the procession winds over cliffs and
under trees with branches layered like the floors
of a building to the hut where the Virgin waits,
dressed in blue and gold, Child in her lap, to
receive the stream of noble visitors. I follow the
figures arranged one behind the next and find
Lorenzo again, in the retinue of the Three Kings. I
try not to wonder what he thinks of now—poetry,
the state of his farmlands, these newly painted
walls, my sister's white skin? I try not to wonder
what he thinks as he glances and then glances
again back at me.

Clarice and Lorenzo lead us out of the chapel,
down the dark stairs and into the courtyard, now
filled with guests who stand circling the bronze
David, his foot delicately placed on the giant's
ugly head. They greet the couple with cheers that
rise up, float out of the palace and over the city
walls to the countryside. One woman wears a hat
of peacock feathers that bob and shimmer as she
waves. Lorenzo stops at the bottom step to show
off his bride. He raises Clarice's hand and makes a
great show of kissing it tenderly, smiling, looking
up into her eyes.

Around the David, the tables are laden with
fruit and casks of wine, with brown roasted geese
and great legs of veal. After the cheering and singing is over, we'll begin the three-day feasting and
the rich odors of meat, the sweet smells of honey
and jam fill the air.

Clarice looks shyly at the guests, but she turns
her head away from the nude David, standing with
hands on boyish hips above the crowd. His chest is
still hairless, very smooth, and he wears a jaunty
hat. My sister is ashamed to look.

The guests part to let us through; they throw flowers, the soft blooms pelting Clarice's face. She has taken Lorenzo's arm but glances briefly—so briefly I am the only one who sees—back at Giuliano who walks beside me. He is busily joking with the young men in the crowd, patting them on the shoulder and whispering things in their ears—no doubt plans for some wilder party later tonight. Clarice catches my eye instead and gives me a strange quivering look as if she's begging me to catch up with them and place my hands at the small of her back—she's always had pains there—but the people press around her, and she smiles at her guests, nods and ducks her head as Lorenzo introduces her to the bankers of Florence. She is lost next to him, huddled beneath his arm, but then she reaches back to me and to our parents to pull us close so that Lorenzo can introduce us too. He is saying something about the David—how his father or grandfather commissioned it from Donatello—but I can't hear because Clarice is nuzzling up to my ear and whispering that no, no, Lorenzo is not how she remembered at all. In between her rustling words, I listen for Lorenzo's—Goliath's winged helmet a symbol of Milan—but that is all I hear. Lorenzo's sisters—Maria, Crezia, and Bianca—take our hands and lead us away from him, off to the banquet.

Determined, slightly wild, Lucrezia is stalking. Her lips are set like a blade across her face. Lorenzo has stopped to speak to a short man with a blue cap, and Clarice stops too, attached to his hand. She watches the words made of lead, brass, gold, clods of earth, leaves, and sky bubble out of his mouth. Soon, husband and wife are both wading through the phrases that gather on the octagonal tiles, pushing them aside with their feet.

In the loggia between courtyard and garden, Clarice and I sit between two of Lorenzo's sisters, and the youngest, Bianca, is down at the other end of the long table entertaining her cousins. There are two hundred young women here, sitting in the pinkish brown shadows cast by the cool stones while the men sit in the courtyard under the hot sun and the older women sit on the balcony above us. Bees fly in from the garden, buzz over the honey pots and carry the strong scent of gardenias. With them, hot bits of breeze like clusters of dandelion seeds float in. Each dish is announced with trumpets and brought to my sister first on a golden tray. She puts one tiny bite after another into her small mouth, not even chewing before she swallows. The sisters, Maria and Crezia, fill and refill our glasses with wine from the large ewers. The tart odor swirls around us.

"Are you happy with the gifts?" I whisper to Clarice, and she nods while taking a long drink of wine. With her finger, she taps the Book of Hours in her lap. It is written in gold letters on blue paper, and the binding covered with designs in crystal and silver. I try to talk lightly about the wedding and the finery of the guests.

"Was that Caterina Strozzi in the hat of peacock feathers?" I ask Maria who sits beside me.

"Oh yes, that famous hat," Crezia says, leaning across Clarice to wink at Maria. As she starts to laugh, her black eyebrows draw together, her cheeks turn a dusty, salmon pink, and she clutches the front of her low-cut dress. She laughs soundlessly until the tears collect and roll from her eyes.

"Just like a peacock trying to attract a hen," Maria says and lays her plump hand on my arm. She's giggling herself. "But Caterina's the wrong sex, and instead of her rump, it's her head she puts the feathers on."

"She seems pleasant," Clarice says. "Such a long face but a beautiful smile."

"Her brother is much better looking," Crezia stammers between gasps for air. "One of our handsomest men."

"Some say he modeled for Donatello," Maria adds, "but he always denies it—a nobleman stripping for an artist, how could anyone think such a thing!" She and her sister begin laughing again, covering their mouths with their hands. I've noticed their teeth are perfectly straight, white, unnaturally long.

"Wouldn't he have modeled for that if he could?" I ask, pointing to the David we can just see glinting between the columns. "It's beautiful work, nothing to be ashamed of." I think of the fresco in the chapel and of Lorenzo's profile hidden behind his father's and grandfather's.

Crezia pours herself more wine, the dark liquid gurgling into her glass. "No one knows who modeled for that," she says.

"Donato and all his pretty boys," Maria mumbles. I hear her but Clarice does not; she's asking Crezia about her own apartments, which direction they face, if they'll get the sun.

Clarice turns away from her sister's nervous fingers that tap on the table and sound like running feet. When Lucrezia was small, she chased the footman from the palazzo around the corner so that she could hear his perfect Tuscan accent, his voice clear and smooth. She would dash out the heavy double doors when she saw him coming, clatter through the courtyard, and follow him down the street. "Speak!" she commanded, pointing up at his mouth, and he would stand at ease, feet apart, hands loosely joined behind his back, eyes rolled up to the blue sky. To please her, he hid his laughter and recited proverbs and recipes and told her stories about his training with one of the noble families of Florence: how, being orphaned, he was taken from their country estate into town and there taught to answer all questions put to him in a deep voice, polite and proper, grammar perfect. She tried to imitate him, to forget the coarse Romano that even her parents spoke at times.

"Ficino too." Maria leans across me, draping her arm over the back of my chair and drawing her own closer. "I hear he still kisses his students on the head while they're studying. He gave Lorenzo great tight hugs when he finished memorizing another verse of Homer." On the other side of Clarice, Crezia also pulls her chair closer. They've made a tight, warm cave around us. Like saints in an altarpiece, the sisters gesture toward us with their limp, long-fingered hands but look away as they speak, down the length of the table. The afternoon shadows have deepened as white paint darkens after many years on the wall. "Your Lorenzo was once quite pretty," Maria says, and Crezia nods as if to tell her sister to continue. Suddenly Clarice looks interested. She turns to Maria and cocks her head.

"Quite pretty before he got into a tussle with Giancarlo Colonna and got his nose broken."

Maria's voice has dropped to a hoarse whisper.
"When they were younger. Still doing their
lessons together."

Clarice sits back and nods, sips her wine. We are
waiting for the sweets and for the servants to clear
the dishes from the white cloth.

"My Lorenzo was once beautiful," she says as if
tasting the words, slowly as if we're not here. She
has her arms crossed loosely in her lap. "I do not
think I would want a handsome man."

She will submit to him tonight. Under him, her
eyes will slide gently over to the side like a Filippo
Lippi Madonna's. He will touch her breasts, push
them into high white mounds one in each hand,
twist them. Later, after he's spent, collapsed onto
her, withdrawn slowly and rolled to his back,
placed one hand beneath his head and the other on
her arm to stop her from drawing up the sheet—
perhaps he'll read her Virgil. My sister's Latin is
excellent, although she doesn't enjoy it as I do.
Once she's asleep, her hands tucked between her
thighs, he may leave her in the gray room, colors
bleached out of the bare, vaulted ceiling, and go to
the party Giuliano is planning. There, the young
men of Florence will unbutton their sodden shirts,
rub their hands over their smooth damp chests in
the cool night breeze, and stretch out languidly on
the grass. Clarice will wake in the morning and
wonder where her husband is.

"Now, you're not saying that our brother is
ugly, are you?" Crezia jokes, and Clarice is quick
to say oh no, of course not, and smiles from one of
her new sisters to the other.

"She looks like Fabriano, doesn't she?" Maria
says across us and then turns to Clarice. "You'll

meet him soon. He's lived here for years. One of Lorenzo's closest friends. Closer than brothers."

"Yes, pale like him—he's so careful of his skin. Whenever he and Lorenzo go riding, he wears a straw hat like a peasant and ties flowers to the ribbon. The same slim hips, too," Crezia says. "Your dress can't hide it, dear. I don't envy you when your first child is due."

Clarice looks like Mother, and she turns to me. We both remember that only five years ago Mother had a son who died soon after birth. Her screams searched us out down the dark corridors to our rooms. We're quiet now, sit back and stretch our legs out beneath the table. The chatter lulls until I can hear the bees again and the clatter of silver in the makeshift scullery just beyond the garden wall. Clarice's hand lies softly in mine with the fingers close together like a kitten's paw.

Lorenzo's crooked nose pushes close and his lips flirt, pretending to touch and then withdrawing until Clarice has to hold his head still, squeeze it between her hands. He smells of sour wine and honey. She will not let him come nearer. His hands shake, touch her hair, inadvertently brush free some pins and the heavy braids fall, unwind, suffocate them. When Clarice looks up, he has turned away and she sees the slant of his forehead and the red curve of his lips close by her. She backs across the bed on her hands and knees, pushing the quilts into a pile with the soles of her feet. Doves coo coo coo outside in the dawn and beat their wings against the glass. When Lorenzo speaks, wine dribbles over his chin, down his neck and chest, unceasing, and stains the sheets—not just a small spot of dirty reddish

*brown. They line up their fingers and he lets her
sleep curled at the foot of the bed.*

Clarice has let her head droop to her chest, but
her eyes are still open. I nudge her when Lorenzo
leads his mother over. Tossing his head, he shakes
his hair loosely from his face. He pats Clarice
lightly on the shoulder and leaves his large hand
there like a strange growth pressing her into the
chair. She touches it with her fingertips as if it
were something precious. Now that they are married, the two more days of celebration seem already to have disappeared. I am on the road back
to Rome, carriage jolting roughly, Mother and
Father nodding across from me, the walls of Florence disappearing behind the hills. My husband
waits in our own home lit with many candles that
spread a warm, soft light. His smile and arms
will be open. There, Florence will be the vaguest
dream, recalled only when I read a letter from my
sister full of gossip and news of her children's first
steps, or see early morning light slant through
haze over the Tiber.

INTERVAL

WALK INTO A STRANGE ROOM and flip the light switch. See a gasp mirrored in surprise. Even after it's clear she's a reflection and not an intruder, she remains disconcerting; turned around, she can't be you. This mirror shows you as others see you—reversed—and not as you're accustomed to seeing yourself in mirrors. When brushing your hair, watch your left hand leave the side of your body and take the brush up to your head, then feel the bristles against your scalp on the right: wrong, wrong. See how crooked the jaw, how uneven the green eyes, the left much larger than the right. Twins could stare like this, primping in front of each other rather than looking in the mirrored door of the medicine cabinet, each turn away with the idea that she is actually the other.

Through all the blue—air, ocean, vault of sky—the white wedge of ship pushed day after day, a near-silent motion of smokestacks, bridge deck, bow splitting waves. Midnight shadows under

white deck chairs, clouds tinged indigo disappeared by sunset. Then, the sun did speckle the
whole sea gold but what it speckled was tur-
quoise, aquamarine, cobalt. Wonderful crossing,
all said, but as if to compensate for the blue, the
cool white of railings and table cloths, and the
sea breeze, the passengers favored warm colors:
a red sweater, a pink dress, peach-colored slip
with satin straps, yellow lace panties, tan knees,
rubies.

"Ness, do you know someone named Franki?"
Jim yelled from the front hall.
"Franki?"
"You got a postcard from someone named
Franki. Whoever that is," he added and tossed it
into the bowl where they threw the mail.
"Franki," she said again and read the message—
a greeting, a description of a trip taken in a rented
car through a foreign country—before turning the
card over to look at the picture of a white wall,
blue curtains, a window that reflected a tree in a
tub, a chair and a rumpled bed rather than showing what was outside.

Across the table, the two women's eyes locked
when the old man began telling a story of natives
putting a bathroom door on backwards, then
laughed until he coughed and choked, his wife
patting his sleeve with her hand, smiling apolo-
getically, delightedly. Telepathy: immediately
they and we. The women found themselves taking
the same side, defending each other against all
others, against the tuxedos and backless evening
dresses that exposed spotted, sagging flesh, to-

gether not laughing at this story until people thought they must already share a life.

Through the porthole the sun fell straight, felled window glass, curtains, hull, so that the cabin filled, dark replaced by a constant light that pushed chair, table, and bed up against the walls. The women's feet braced footboard then head-board, toes curling around cold metal. Skin, bodies rolling, flattened creased sheets, crunched them again into a ball.

Vanessa saw crimson swirl like blood down a drain, but Franki tugged at her lashes until she opened her eyes, saw bright red hair, body spark, freckles. In the cabin, light made white a fire, can-celled blue, cancelled all previous pledges.

"The man sitting next to you reminded me of someone," Vanessa said after introductions, for-malities, but every man she met reminded her of other men she'd been with: a torn earlobe, licked lips, bristles of hair shaved on the back of the neck, the way one had of clutching her in public and pressing himself against her thigh—all these qualities adhered to the new man, gathered like iron filings on a magnet and made him harder to know. She described the last man too, the one she'd left to come on this trip. "But I don't care about him anymore," she said.

"You remind me of no one," Franki thought. She felt her smile stiffen. With the telling of a new tale, Vanessa's face changed color, shape, one moment to the next. These were secrets told much too soon, but Franki didn't leave, just shifted slightly, held to her seat.

At other tables conversation rose, rolled out through the dim room without breaking. They were trapped whole inside their bodies like specimens in jars, bounded by the soft green light of the lamp hanging over them, the glass walls holding tables and chairs in place, and in the dark, the Atlantic surrounding the ship—enclosure within enclosure.

In the city they moved from one sublet to another, tried all the neighborhoods, but nowhere did the sun barrel into the rooms. Or perhaps they were never home at the right time, and the midday or setting sun fell straight through their windows, stumbled across chairs and spilled dresser drawers without being seen. "Vanessa's mess," Franki said when she came in late from work, then shut the bedroom door because they were having company again. Vanessa brought someone home almost every night; the others, they watched the news on TV, read the paper silently after supper.

"My roommate," Vanessa said, holding her arm out, her hand pointing limply in Franki's direction while her guest took off his jacket. On the best china, the set they'd just found in the hall closet, they served curried prawns, and while they ate, Jim complimented them on the apartment, the food, the wine.

"We've lived so many places this year, I can't keep them straight," Franki said. "We'd really like to have a place of our own." She waited for Jim to say "What do you mean? I thought this was Vanessa's place," but he only grunted a bit and scooped up more rice and peas with his fork. She expected Vanessa to protest; she just smiled, silent.

Later, out on the narrow balcony, after the sun had set, Vanessa showed her guest the view, curtsied, laughed, sidled up to him, their talk muffled by the door closed to keep out the hot summer air. While she cleared the table, Franki watched the two of them lean over the rail, shoulder to shoulder, to see the shimmer of the river down at the end of the street. Wretched, she could simply step out, pick them up by the ankles and tip them over so they did flip after flip before landing, two sacks of broken bones, busted and bloody. She saw them tumbling through the gray evening until she felt her own stomach turn over, shivered, left the thought behind when she went to wash the dishes. In the kitchen she clanked forks against pots and pans. To think that Vanessa kept pointing out landmarks as if she'd always lived here! Franki couldn't remember which set of sheets was on this bed, which belonged to the last bed they'd slept in, which print hung in this bathroom and which in another. She couldn't straighten it out, countless rooms and clutter. When she went to join the others on the balcony, she was sure that, as she slid open the doors, the man and woman stepped apart.

Folding the postcard, Vanessa slipped it into her wallet behind photos of Bernard, Jerry, Richard, Zachary. Flipping these others aside—there was Franki, her hair the color of stripped electrical wire, a smile of big white teeth. Her face was a mask just as it had always been to Vanessa. If she decided to look into Franki's eyes, this snapshot would tell nothing, not even her own desire.

Despite Vanessa's wildness . . . Not wildness,

no, Franki corrected herself, for each of those many expressions was carefully planned or had been until they became a part of her. No, Vanessa was self-contained, unapproachable behind a squat glass of whiskey though she might be smiling over it with her eyes, a wall whose nature it is to stand solidly festooned with wild roses and yet dares you to pull it down.

But after several, after many glasses of whiskey in the ship's saloon or at home sitting over the table, staring out the window, Vanessa's outline began to blur, to shift and double, and her whole being became like a woman's back—disheveled, unbrushed hair splayed across a red dress with hundreds of tiny buttons undone and the fabric crumpled, like the back of a woman Franki might see standing by the door at a party and try to reach only to keep being interrupted, stopped for drinks and talk so that, just as she was ready to begin pushing through the crowd again, she realized the woman had moved and was now hidden behind someone else: a woman who tried but was never able to reach behind far enough to slip the buttons through the buttonholes, as if, for the first time, Franki could see her own back. Then, Vanessa's essence, the search for words, for a cigarette, became this repetitive struggle to find the buttons, forgetting they needed to be fastened, then remembering and reaching around again to pull the tangled dirty hair aside and fit a few buttons through the wrong holes in an attempt to pull herself together. And between the two halves of the creased red dress, the skin was delicate, stretched tautly over the shoulder blades, so white and brittle it could be paper, exposed, startling, but Franki recognized it immediately, the way one recognizes a smell from home.

Even as Vanessa promised that she was relinquishing the past, all the unmatched socks in a bottom drawer, something tugged at her, suggesting she might be lying, that she would change her mind again. Later, she wondered how Franki could have changed so quickly: a street-corner game of three-card monte with love the distraction, flip and slip of numbers, colors, faces—gone. If only they'd taken more time, hadn't spent all that time watching the sea sliding under the damp white sheets of cloud without talking.

Touch. Franki's hand shook. She watched Vanessa's ear and cheek, watched Vanessa watching wave after blue wave slosh, shshsh, through white porthole ring. Then, turning suddenly, Vanessa knocked Franki's hand aside, painfully, where it had just reached up and out.

Lace blouse, high collar unbuttoned for her, Franki had seen herself in the mirror but this, now, must be someone else's body, warmer.

Voices. Hers? Theirs? Outside? No, silence banked against door, walls, insulated ceiling and floor. Eyes unfocused so there was only a blur of pale face, this room, this bed. Whisper and hiss of fingers burrowing in flesh.

They found new jobs, moved to the country, to a perfect glass rectangle of a house set in the middle of the forest, a bare and empty house where they looked out and saw green, blue. At first sleep came easily. They followed the sun from corner to corner. Later, they turned up the radio at night, pushed the few pieces of furniture aside, and danced with their eyes closed, a glass in one hand and a cigarette in the other, each moving to a separate insistent beat. Only when the morning paper hit the door and fell to the step did they look at each other. They saw the pale gray winter light chink between the curtains and the paper boy outside shielding his eyes, looking in at their sweaty disorder, their knotted hair, smudged make-up, the bra straps fallen around their upper arms. They fumbled, emptied ashtrays as if cleaning up after a perfectly normal party.

Days when even the continuous pressure of the ship through the air didn't disturb the heat, everyone pulled themselves around the deck by holding on to the railings. Listlessly, they followed the shade from one awning to another, gathering in the cool absence of color. They sipped drinks that made the glasses sweat. Holding a damp paper napkin to her cheek, Vanessa waited for Franki to come by, knowing she'd be walking briskly, ignoring the sun, her sleeves buttoned tightly at the wrist.

If the evening were at all windy, Franki buttoned her blouse up to her chin, pulled on a sweater, then a jacket, and knotted a scarf around her neck while others removed still more layers of clothing, welcoming the chill on their skin. Inside, Vanessa wondered, inside among heart, liver, kidneys, spleen all pumping, secreting, cleansing, did Franki have another organ, small and delicate, that couldn't stop trembling? Franki was forgetful too, absent-minded even, despite the fact that she had a crease ironed down every sleeve and gathered all her hair into a heavy, neat bun. When she came in from the deck for a game of cards, she left her jacket in the corner of a sofa, her scarf thrown over the arm of a chair and a sweater sliding off the seat, arms dangling. Later, once everyone had gone to bed and Franki, yawning, disappeared, Vanessa picked up these pieces of clothing, folded them, piled them where Franki would be sure to find them in the morning not even aware she had left them behind until she saw them there. Vanessa handled the wool, silk, cotton, fascinated with these leavings, as if they were a skin that, in being shed, revealed an essential, frightened, fragile, familiar self.

"Maybe we could have maintained the illusion," Franki thought, "if we'd come to this house right away. Maybe then I wouldn't always be itching, scratching, shaking myself to get rid of something crawling on my skin that turns out to be my skin itself. Maybe if we'd driven straight from the ship blindfolded, through the city and up the interstate as if we were being taken to a hideout where kidnappers held people we loved and we had to get there as quickly as possible without saying anything to anyone in order to save them."

Blue. Night. The moon rose and shone fine and silvery, slivered by bars, railings, and steps, slid between decks like a secret. Light sliced water but they didn't see silver, moon, sea, bright knife, or only looked through these to each other, saying "See moon, sea, silver." Kiss-kiss of water against the ship.

"Open a window," Franki said, but the windows

in the house didn't open, and if they had, humid
summer heat would only have replaced the cool
stale air inside. She lay back on the couch, eyes
closed, trying to breathe. Pictures flashed: spine
bumpy through white skin, black water, tangled
hair, a dress undone as if forgotten but hardened
that way into a shield and a studied seduction.

Franki sees glass walls, empty, reflecting flick-
ering leaves, clouds, sky. She didn't see Vanessa
standing at the end of the driveway, watching her,
but had to stop, steady herself against the car
before lifting her bags into the trunk. Behind her:
the glass house built to preserve the fine blues and
startling light of the ocean cruise like a ship in a
bottle.

The stillness presses on her; Vanessa's turned
all the lights on but nothing moves shadows. At
night, late, the armchairs and standing lamps with
bell-shaped shades receded into the dark, away
from her, leaving each room a vastness, creaking
with her steps. She wandered through doorways
that were black holes in gray walls, pushed aside
drapes to see the great night-light of the city outside, checking to make sure windows were closed
against the thunderstorm she'd felt coming on
when she'd stepped out of the taxi, the hazy
yellow of streetlamps, muted, far below.

In the bedroom, Franki slept all angles of elbows, knees, chin, wrists, dark twist of limbs on
the sheet, one leg flung across the other. That day,
she'd cut all her hair off, a red weight, and what
was left was soft, thin, worn like the nap on an old
carpet. Vanessa lifted Franki's head from the pillow, but she didn't wake. She pressed the bony
irregularities of Franki's skull—ridges behind the

ears, indentation at the top of the neck—between her palms, but still Franki didn't wake, just sat up in her sleep and threw herself down the other way, thumping against the mattress and sighing. Then she sat again, eyes still closed, and pulled the blankets up, covering herself spread diagonally over the bed. Vanessa went back to the living room, woke hours later, years later, cramped on the couch.

AFTERIMAGE

IT'S A HILL like a fan that takes Daniel Vorst down to town. It's the largest hill on the island, and its ridges and roads run down to town like pleats. They meet at a point at the post office— Stonington, Maine 04681. On the other side of town the water fans out again larger and larger. First there is the harbor speckled with lobster boats. Then there is the bay speckled with islands. The boats and islands are like dots on a stocking: the dots of the boats are on the ankle, small and close together; the dots of the islands are on the thigh, larger and spread apart. At the mouth of the bay, the water fans out into the Atlantic and all the way to Europe.

Daniel Vorst lives just on the other side of the hill, just as the land dips down and starts rolling to the water again. He can't see the water though, for his house is surrounded by locust trees, maple trees, spruce trees, and alders that choke the old apple trees. There are no beech trees although this is Beech Hill. Even in early spring before the leaves open, the trees are so thick that they hide everything from the house.

Since the middle of winter, Daniel Vorst has lived alone. An image governed the move to this island: he saw himself inside the low-ceilinged rooms of the farmhouse looking out at the pines black against the snow and then turning in again, away from the window, to sit down with a book alone. He has been here since the beginning of January in voluntary seclusion.

At first he kept the radio on at all times and talked to it. Now, in April, he talks only to himself. He exchanges few words with the shopkeepers in town, says "thank you" when given the change for his purchases, mentions the sudden warmth of the sun, and asks for his mail in a voice slow, hushed, and rough. "Anything for Vorst?" he asks every day, but he gets almost nothing— bills and a rare postcard of a different ocean from his daughter. He shoves them into his jacket pocket, puts his box of groceries on the back seat of his car, and drives home, keeping his eyes on the gray sky, the black pines, the white birches. Back at the house the thin light filters through branches into the rooms and is gone by four o'clock. Daniel sits, left in the circle of light from a lamp, bent over a book at the dining room table. He is perfectly still; the light settles around his shoulders.

■　■　■

Early spring comes in April when the road turns to mud and the weather is milder but still raw— more wet than cold. In six weeks the lilacs may be in bloom. It's on one of these raw days that Daniel lets that fanlike hill take him down to town on foot. "The road to town has three stages," Daniel says as he starts out. "First there is the slow descent out of the trees and through the blueberry field. Second there is the steep walk down through the forest on the other side of the field. Third there is the walk through town itself, down along Main Street which runs by the harbor."

ONE

Brown mud coats the narrow road and slides down the steepest parts of the hill back toward the house. Daniel, following the road, is dressed in brown and his hair is gray as the sky. Above him the trees arch and the wind cracks the black branches together. The night's rain kicked up the smell of last fall's rotten leaves. Ditches follow the twists and turns of the road, and the water in them rustles and rushes past Daniel.

At the top of the ridge, the highest point on the island, the trees give way to the low clouds that hover but obscure nothing and to the blueberry field, a sudden expanse of brownish land studded with boulders dropped by a retreating glacier now located somewhere north of Hudson Bay. The boulders mark the field like buoys marking the entrance to the Thoroughfare, and the road wends through them, keeping some to the right and others to the left just as a boat would.

From here the hill rushes down to town and out into the bay, and Daniel stops to watch it. At his feet are the tiny, brittle, leafless branches of the wild berry bushes. Further on, the dead grass hides them, and further still, the gray and black trees of the forest replace the grass and roll on down the hill. The white houses beyond the trees and the boats in the harbor are brilliantly lit with a stark and unearthly light, fluorescent against the deep gray of the bay—iron and smoke and steel. Spread out on the water, each of the islands is perfectly clear, perfectly etched black. This is the view from the top of Beech Hill, the view that's scattered before Daniel Vorst and that the wind blows into his face so fiercely he must close his eyes.

It's so broad he can't see it all. He always thought the frames around the windows of his car kept him from seeing the rim of the world to the southeast and the lumpy hills of the mainland off to the north at the same time. Today though, when he's on foot, he still can't see both the furrowed sky above and the cars driving back and forth in town below. He can't watch a man head into the drugstore and the whole world at once.

At Daniel's feet each detail of the dry vegetation resolves against the wet ground—the knobby joints of forked twigs, the frayed ocher grass knotted like intricate twists of tangled hair. When he looks up again, he gasps for breath. The bay tips up; the islands slide toward him. He recoils, lowering his head and following the ruts in the road to town.

TWO

Daniel Vorst's in the forest again where the trees close in and the wind rattles the branches above his head. As he walks down the hill the breaks between the trees increase. He glances through them and up the muddy driveways to the boats sitting in dry dock and the lobster traps piled like cages on the lawns.

The breaks between the trees accelerate, thirty-two feet per second, gathering speed on the way to town. Although he braces himself against the steep descent, Daniel, too, gathers speed. His own weight pulls him bolting down the hill, and the forest and road flash by, a blur. The houses streak the gray wall of trees white. He hears a young woman calling from one of them to a dog and sees her solid form in an open doorway—her flowered house dress stretched tight across her belly, her white arm flung wide—but he swings past her around the bend, and the answering barks of the dog grow fainter and deeper as he watches the road for rocks and races to town. His heart beats triple time. Gravity's got him, pulling him toward the bay. The water's out there, flat and still and far. The water's close now; transparent waves slosh against the dock at Daniel's feet.

THREE

Daniel walks by the closed motel and the green-shingled movie house with the string of blue bulbs outside on his way down Main Street. It runs along the edge of the harbor, and the stinking mud flats can be seen between the buildings. He passes no one, but in the post office he finds the woman in the red suit. She's the only one there besides Elma Eaton, the postmistress. She's tall and plump and her suit has a close-fitting jacket and a tight skirt. Redder than the skin of strawberries, it's the reddest red Daniel can think of. In the white post office under the gray sky, it blazes. Daniel has never seen this woman before but Elma seems to know her and, as always, stands behind the stamp window shaking her gray curls as she talks. Shifting his weight, impatient, Daniel stands to the side.

"What can this red suit possibly be doing in this town?" he thinks.

With a raised finger, Elma signals to Daniel to wait. She tells the woman in the red suit about Sally Greenfield, and the woman nods her head piled high with hair the color of teak and says, "So sad. I didn't know," over and over. It's news to Daniel too.

"You've heard, haven't you? The funeral's tomorrow. She was so young, only seventeen, and the baby was with her." While Elma talks, a man comes into the post office and stands behind the woman in the red suit. He looks down at her legs and so does Daniel: the dots on her stockings are close together on the ankle and spread further apart on the calf. She turns around to see who it is and smiles warmly. "It was still strapped into its seat when they pulled the car out of the water." Daniel watches the woman's white hand at the end of that red sleeve reach around behind her and join with the wrinkled and dirty hand of the man. He is old enough to be her father, her grandfather even, but their fingers are busily twining like python and prey, like lovers' legs. "She was going down that hill by the movie house that's so steep. You know, I've been saying for years they should put a guardrail at the bottom. It heads straight into the harbor, and that's just what Sally did too." Even once the fingers have come to rest in a stevedore's knot, a harness hitch, or a studding sail halyard bend, Daniel thinks he can see the sparks fly. She is flint, he is steel. "Right into the water. I don't suppose a guardrail would have helped much. High tide, you know. The baby with her and everything. It was a wet day, but Bud Greenfield says he never had any trouble with the brakes on that car before he gave it to his daughter."

Finally, Daniel looks up again. He can't watch their hands and see their faces at the same time. "So many untimely deaths this year," Elma says. "Just last November Billy Haskell drowned when he was out scalloping. He was up fixing the winch when he slipped." Daniel looks at the hands that must be knotting and unknotting on their own for the woman in the red suit is listening carefully with the same concerned look in her eyes. "The sea was rough, but even if it weren't, that water's likely to freeze you the minute you fall in. He was the baby's father, but he wouldn't marry Sally. I know it happens all the time. Even when I was young." The man is waiting quietly for the conversation to end as if he, like Daniel, wants to pick up his mail and buy a few stamps. "Such a shame. She was planning to go off to school at Machias and be a teacher."

Daniel looks back at the woman in the red suit and something about her face has changed. It's glowing now like her suit, not red but luminous, bleached clamshell white. She's smiling that same small smile but now that smile's ready to break its bounds. Her face is full of pleasure, of joyous expectation. He sees it run a blue streak from the hand behind her joined with the man's hand, up the red sleeve of her jacket, through her heart to her face. It seems she is standing at the point of a pink granite ledge with the gray water surging at her feet, ready to go. Listening to these tales of death, he watches as if two clasped hands were utterly new to the world.

■ ■ ■

Later, after buying cod for dinner at the Fish Co-op, Daniel walks out on to the pier. Scales and slime gleam in rainbow colors, iridescent on the wooden boards. Before him, the bay spreads out, strewn with islands. Off to the south, the ocean extends to the end of the world. He can see the line where gray water meets gray sky while the same wind that pushes the clouds and slaps the water against the pilings blows in his face.

From behind Sheep Island, the *Mary Ellen* is coming in, her wake fanning out, white, behind her. She pulls up to the pier, gulls circling overhead, and her men unload an already headless and gutless fish the length of a man on to the conveyor belt.

"What's that?" Daniel asks a young man walking away in his thigh-high boots.

"Tuna," he says, "Hundred pounder," and joins the other men who are laughing, some of them toothlessly, and slapping each other's yellow waterproof backs.

"Hundred pounder," Daniel thinks, looking at the fish's dark blue back and the fins and finlets running to the tail, enough to feed a hundred and fifty people, maybe even more. He thinks of all eating at once, seated around a white-clothed table.

The wind is charged now, and the whitecaps run in toward shore. Daniel stands wide-eyed at the ragged edge of the boards and watches the trawlers listing out on the bay, the tiny figures on their decks stretching out and leaning back as they haul in the heavy nets under the scudding clouds.

Behind him, he feels the woman in the red suit approach and feels her hands touch his own. He is waiting, and in the wind, he feels his body start to sway.

DIORAMAS

*LANDSCAPE IS NO REDEMPTION but a
curse, a bore, a story we tell ourselves at four in
the morning—no matter what anyone says. That
postcard—it's here somewhere—awful reproduction of the Freidrich painting where a man in a
frock coat stands poised at the brink and looks
over a sublime prospect of mountain tops lost in
fog. Earth and air move rapturously together;
white mist pushes against the crags, spreads
through the abyss. Now there's a fine example of
landscape for you. Don't groan as if you can't
stand to think of it; I've caught you staring at it
often enough. You'll burn a hole in the cardboard
with that look. But if we could see the man's face,
maybe we'd see that he's bored, that he's just a
model doing his job. No, of course not. How silly
of me. Of course it's impossible to see his face.*

*Visions. Places we've seen or maybe imagined.
How about the cemetery we used to walk in? A
beautiful place but one tired of it so easily if one
wasn't in the right mood; the ride home on the
express bus past bakeries and drugstores came as*

137

*a relief. That spot was charming though, planned
as carefully as an English garden: all that's most
delightful in nature arranged in a series of small
surprises. You liked it, you can't tell me you
didn't. We avoided funerals and picked out our
stones, keeping to the gravel paths and the short
stiff grass beneath the elms. With each step,
a different vista came into view—a miniature
temple to Apollo, gazebos, a sea captain with his
spyglass, the lion lying down with the lamb.
Shadows of leaves flickered on the lawns. The
white stones dotting the greensward glowed in
the late afternoon sun as we tried to choose
among them, imagining our death: Beloved,
Faithful, and the dates. We thought of adopting
one that stood at the crest of a hill and boasted
separate markers for husband and wife. From
each, a marble arm reached out and the hands
clasped eternally; remember, he held hers in a
mighty grip. Something grander might be even
more appropriate, but we've settled for a simple
stone with a brief admonishment, all that's nec-
essary we've realized.*

*Come, these thoughts will never let us sleep.
Turn on the lamp so you can see yourself in the
dark window against the rain, reach for the
switch under the pink shade painted with daisies
and rearing horses. The wind rips and screeches,
even down these tight streets, and it tangos the
garbage in the empty lot on the corner. What can
you see? Yourself: woman in the glass nodding
uncontrollably, nose widened out of proportion,
cheekbones spread apart as if by insistent hands,
skin dull and crinkled as brown paper bags. Light
shatters the earrings, necklace, and rhinestone
crown we settle atop scant gray hair. Though we*

are no longer as young as we once were, we are just as much in need of amusement and solace. Come now, pull the purple velvet around your shoulders for warmth. There are worse places than this room with its Naugahyde armchair, single bed that cranks up and down, private bath with Dixie cup dispenser full of fluted white cups for urine samples and drinks of water. And better.

After midnight: talk; take up the coverlet we're knitting, each square a different pattern—jacquard diamonds, Vandyke swag, four-color blister, Dura-Europas, and Rapunzel's braid; sit over the card table scrubbed clean and ready for imprint; spread paper over bare earth, tower the books, pave the streets between them with brushes and pencil stubs; use fingers with nails thick as wood to stir the ink and paint and pools of color for eyes, mouth, cheeks. Come. Play. Govern this empire. Begin to speak. Outline Urals and Pyrenees, the tattered wave on a Sinhalese beach, the wrought iron fence of a city park, and scrawl in words to people these with color as if leaving instructions. Ignore failing eyesight and trace brows, lips, nose, a face different but still your own. Each book, picture, or thought turns a tale as a potter's hands form clay. Landscape could be the story of our life; it keeps us awake with an infinite sadness told and retold by tears or with the intensity of a pleasure drawn out, wrung dry by dawn.

I

The boy watched, followed, watched. His eyes sank into his pinched face and the fuzz went unshaved on his cheeks. Though he couldn't move or look away, she danced around the island with ease. She knew the place as well as the half-moon imprint of her own foot in the sand, how the land split a stream of warm water. On it, the eucalyptus trees grew densely, providing shade and some relief from the heat, their sharp medicinal smell not quite overpowering the mud. That was her own smell; the shape of the island, the shape of her tears.

In the heat she walked around naked, but the air was murky as dusty voile and the trees dropped yards of dark shadow along with their slim, saber-shaped leaves. He had to strain to see her sometimes, and in order to be able to do so no matter where she went, he sat at the center of the island with his knees clasped to his chest and his chin resting between them, watching her the way he might watch a colony of ants—with dogged fascination. But he was afraid of her too, impassive and nervous at the same time; when she came up to him, he flinched.

"I look for a tree that isn't a tree but flits between them. I listen for a songbird with a voice sweeter than any I've heard before, one that darts more swiftly between the leaves than a hummingbird, or I follow the scurrying of a small animal that's lighter than a squirrel. That's where you are," he whispered hoarsely when she asked him how he'd developed the ability to stare through tree trunks to find her. He stared all the time—at her brown arms and legs, breasts, the rough soles of her feet when she squatted to wash her face, at her ankles. He thought of her as a proper lady lifting her skirts a bit to keep from stepping on them.

She circled the island, checking on her domain, the jade trees and purple fuschias on the sandy banks, the spires of the bridge upstream standing like two dead pines against the sky. At shore she watched the blue river, wide and inviting as a bed, but she could still feel his eyes: amazing, the power of his gaze, like a rope around her neck. "I'll break it," she thought, took a quick, shallow dive starting from absolute stillness and swam down into the cool where the red sand turned to red rock and the weeds swirled in the eddies slinky as nightclub hostesses. Even there though, she thought of him. "I can just see him. He's not quite sure what to do. He's beginning to wonder what happened to me." She smiled.

He started to get up, involuntarily, but sat down again, afraid that she'd reappear on another beach while he wasn't looking. He missed her already. He knew he could have gone down to the shore with her and taken a swim or looked at the stars at night; she goaded him often enough but he preferred the grove of trees even if it did smell of wet ashes and mold. He knew he'd gotten thin and pale but his passion tied him to that one spot, and he knew, too, that despite these weaknesses there was one thing she appreciated: his fingers were as deft and nimble as the long green toes of the lizards that sunned themselves on the rocks. Down at a deep spot in the river, she imagined him rustling the strips of bark and the cone-shaped eucalyptus berries with those fingers to distract himself while she was gone. Looking up through the water, she expected to see his skinny hands playing with the leaves the way the wind did, as if he were withering away to nothing but wind, but she only saw her own hair turning back and forth above her head and thought maybe she'd bring back a present—a pretty pebble, a handful of sand, or a stick twisted into a funny shape by the river. He'd cradle and cuddle it as if it were a part of her while she stood back and tried not to laugh.

"I could leave this place as easy as that," she thought sometimes, snapping her fingers, "just wade across the shallows and be gone." She was in control. Other days, she looked around and remembered to sweep the fallen branches into a pile, to shore up the rocks displaced from the levee at the north end of the island, to trim the dead flowers from the wild roses. She belonged to the place. She felt responsible though she was no older than he and kept hoping he'd make a move that had nothing to do with her, turn his head away, exercise his thin neck, anything that showed he could fend for himself. She dreamed that if he did, she'd stay then too—happily—and they'd walk around their island together, slowly at first but freely.

II

"Exquisite! So very exquisite," he told his friends, but he only told them because they asked. He'd gone as a tourist and was expected to greet the unusual with wonder. He repeated the things he'd taught himself to say: they left the coastline behind where they'd looked around a cyclorama of subtle shadings of gray—ashen water, dove gray sky, silvery ice, and the pearl of illusion—then sledded through snowstorms where the flakes were ivory characters playing on a screen of white and over glaciers where their dark glasses failed to keep the sun from slicing through the day. At times the glaciers had split before them, revealing caves of ice; inside, the ice had been blue as the sky, and the light green as if they were under water which, as their guide pointed out, they were. The cold had accompanied them everywhere, crept under their furs, down, and wool even on the brightest days. It was a dry, constant cold that froze the breath inside their nostrils, and if they stopped moving for an instant, shivering started in their extremities, rocking their bones together. One person on the trip insisted on telling stories of Arctic explorers who had taken their frozen fingertips off with their gloves. After his friends had gasped at these tales of frostbitten ears and frozen lungs, he lowered his voice dramatically and proceeded to describe crumpled oceans of ice, jumbled sheets of it tossed by the sea as easily as evening papers blown about in the gutter, a sky bluer at midday than the purest precious stone, the sun low on the horizon giving each crystal of ice its own purple shadow in the bright dust-free air, glories unlike anything he'd ever seen at lower latitudes. Those were some of the things he said when asked about his trip, and he did not believe any of them were actually false.

"What about that blonde you met?" his friends broke in and asked. They'd been introduced to her at a party and imagined the two of them had zipped their sleeping bags together in their shared tent like teenagers on a class trip. They smiled, patted his head, jabbed him playfully in the ribs with their elbows, but he did not tell them how each evening, or what had passed for evening there, she and he had played cards and kept careful score; they'd let the sun circle the horizon on its own, then closed their eyes to sleep while the bruised skies of sunset and dawn followed each other. He found talking to his friends more tiring than any expedition, and when they asked yet

again how he'd withstood the great cold, he did
not bother to answer that after only a day or two,
even the cold became monotonous, something to
resign oneself to for the duration, there no longer
being any mystery in it, or that once summer
arrived, the tundra was mild as a prairie in April.
He did not describe how, to everyone on the trip
except the guide who kept up a facade of unflag-
ging interest, all the mountains of snow had soon
seemed to be the same mountain against an end-
lessly clear sky, the snow blanker than any lake
water, lacking even the motion of the smallest
waves. The herds of musk-ox browsing the short
grass seemed to be the same herd no matter where
their guide led them, and they'd grown to feel that
they stared, constantly, at a single view, a vista so
bright they squinted until they saw only a blur of
light.

"Spectacular, spectacular," he said and breathed
very deeply. For his friends, or these people he'd
always considered, so innocently, his friends, that
seemed to be enough; they were willing to accept
a wonder that could not be described as long as
they believed at least one of them had experienced
it. He did not tell them that even the most spectacular scenery could be dull, that things being so
apparently the same had not caused him to pay
more mind to the minutiae surrounding him, to
find cause for delight in the soaring of a Thayer's
gull for example. The trip had indeed been spectacular but perhaps because the landscape was so
alien as to be overwhelming; he was only beginning to realize this himself, and shortly, as he
grew accustomed to the idea, he hoped his memo-
ries might mesh more closely with the stories he

told, a truth he might have the courage to say caught in the matrix.

When it snowed at home, the girl he'd met came over. They dealt the cards out at the kitchen table and as they played, said every word they'd ever learned in any language for winter weather, including the twenty-seven Eskimo words for snow they never could apply, being unable to recognize the fine distinctions in the world they referred to. They repeated the words until they no longer had any notion of what they were saying; each sound took on life, fluttering around the room, and they could only toss down their cards and roll to the floor with laughter, irrepressible, unconfined. There, in the presence of refrigerator and range, they shook, staggered with awe.

III

Once, for almost two years, she lived in a stone house set back from a road repaved and patched like a crazy quilt. She left a city where the buildings leaned in toward the centers of the streets until she thought their cornices would fall, where people crowded the sidewalks, avoiding puddles of slush at the curb and slapping their hands fitfully against the bricks as they walked. In all that dizzy motion, she searched for a still spot but she felt that the corners of every otherwise empty and lonely room housed intruders, ghosts, filing cabinets stuffed with deeds, wills, diaries. Craving silence, she took the money—whatever she had— and got out. It was still possible to rent something cheap in the country then as long as the setting wasn't too picturesque, and after seeing numerous places, she agreed to take a gray house, squat and unprotected in the middle of some fields fenced off from the property with barbed wire. She saw little beauty there, but the land did stretch away to a distant ridge of bluish hills with only a line of short trees along the road to break up the space. When she looked doubtfully at the bit of ground around the house, the agent assured her that the previous tenants had raised tomatoes, beans, and lettuce successfully, and that the surrounding fields were all planted with lavender. A few weeks later when she moved in, they were already a haze of green, and she felt glad to be alone in the midst of such plenty.

Two chimneys stuck up like thumbs from the slate roof and were the first things she saw when she rounded the bend on the way from town. The driveway led straight to the stoop and ended in a rutted parking place, but out back she began to work with a pick and crowbar to loosen the stones from her plot of land, carried pails of water from the pantry tap, watched the leaves unfurl through the dirt, only occasionally bothering to look up at what lay beyond her fence. She went back and forth between garden and house, exploring happily. The front door opened with a creak and shut abruptly, pulled by its own weight. Inside, the rooms had low, crooked ceilings, whitewashed walls, and one or two windows set deep into the stone. Each pane framed an abstraction that changed with the seasons, and that first summer wide layers of green, purple, and blue filled them. Once in a great while, a swallow plunged through the air, or the vertical of a man disrupted the pure horizontals of land and sky as he walked the rows, moving with suppleness and grace, bending, checking the plants. She left all the windows open, though they let in the heat, so that the odor of lavender and the continuous hum of bees would fill the rooms along with the rich green-gold light. In town she bought postcards of the purple fields with squares on the back that could be scratched with a fingernail to smell the perfume. She wrote to everyone she knew: This is life here—a terrible sweetness.

In the fall she stood at the front door and noted how effortlessly the tractors turned the soil. She watched the geese fly south and the clouds close over the earth; with the grayness, the horizon contracted around the house. At the moment when light sank away, the farmhands walked past her mailbox, the same three men every night. She leaned against the post and waited for them to tip their hats so she could nod in return, a conversation of gestures. Sometimes she spoke with the eldest man whose voice was deep and hollow. If the others started to flirt or gossip about their employer, he shut them up by cuffing them with his gloves. She smiled at this give-and-take, but once they slouched around the curve with their hands in their hip pockets, they were wiped clean from her memory, and she went inside to a meal of the vegetables she'd grown, taking her time, watching the stars fill the kitchen window while she ate, like diamonds poured from an open palm into a jewel box.

That winter she felt a peace in the spread of muddy ground occasionally covered with snow, the smell of wood smoke from the fire, the quiet streets of the town where she did her shopping. She spent her time refinishing furniture she found in the attic, plastering and painting walls, or simply walking from room to room looking out the windows until the separate slices of brown earth and gray sky spun into a single panorama. In the afternoons she often sat with her back to the window and read the books she ordered through catalogs, her head casting a dark shadow on the white pages. She read aloud, savoring, although she did not realize it at the time, the rhythms and inflections of voices other than her own.

By February, though, she began to think the vegetables she brought up from the freezer tasted watery and pale as if she had pushed them too far with her weeding, prodding, fertilizing. By late March she decided to plant cypresses by the front door, or rather, she saw the tall twisted trees in the nursery and immediately envisioned them like streaks of ink against the stones, providing long lines of shade on the lawn. One day after a rain she dug the holes for them, the ground and roof steaming in the unusual spring heat. While she rested before lowering the trees, a man appeared in the mist, walking over the still-bare fields toward her house. Though he wore a cap with the brim snapped back just as the other farmhands did, she recognized his height and the peculiar shuffling gait that distinguished him from the younger men. He climbed the fence, swinging his leg wide of the barbed wire, and hopped down.

"Figured I'd pitch in," he said, and paused. "I saw you starting to plant and I knew you didn't have anyone to help."

Later they drank tea together in the kitchen. She sipped from her cup and watched the light in his face marking every line and fold.

"Yesterday when you were at the window, you looked just like this calendar girl I got a picture of. I brought it to show you." He pulled out the damp yellowed photo he meant—a girl behind glass spotted with rain. She tried to feel flattered that he thought of her as so young and blond, but she knew it was the pensiveness he meant to compare even if he didn't say so.

"Why that doesn't look a bit like me," she joked. With someone else there, the room seemed fuller to her and yet more spacious, as if it grew with company. She noticed things she hadn't paid attention to since moving in: the shadow of the colander rich as leopard skin, the row of bright copper pots hanging unused against the wall. He'd washed his hands, brushing all the dirt out from under his nails, and taken off his muddy shoes to preserve her freshly swept floors.

Once summer came again with its color and heat, the planting done and the crop established, he courted her, calling early in the morning so they could walk through the fields together. Up and down the rows they promenaded, their heads bent. Sometimes he chided her, slapping her wrist if she reached out to touch the waist-high flowers, warning her of the pesticides sprayed on them, and they both laughed nervously, all the talking they did. Late in the day they sat at the kitchen table with glasses of lemonade. He pushed his hat back on his gray head. As he told her slowly about the farm he was born on and the other farms he'd worked, she waited for something to bloom, trying to discern a language in the movements of his large, awkward hands. That he talked at all came as a surprise, and if she could respond, that surprised her even more.

They spent the winter in the parlor, sitting across the wood stove from each other, bent to different tasks. Compulsively, he whittled until he had nothing but a pile of chips that he then, meticulously, swept from the floor. He washed dishes, folded linen, played solitaire in his pajamas for hours every morning. At times—often, in fact—they were driven by their bodies, groping though without joy. Clouds smothered the roof. Over the fields the fog closed in as it had the winter before, though it seemed oppressive to her now rather than ethereal. The cypresses scratched the bedroom window as planned; she listened, closed her eyes, and tried to think of their bodies as precious and perfect despite their frailties, their age. Combined, they did not reach a hundred but they both seemed ancient to her, as if each limb had been tested by thousands of lovers before and each time had been found more wanting than the last. They fumbled, failed passion, performed the actions by rote, achieved meager satisfaction.

Tedium weighed on her though she barely noticed its advance, the way dust will settle on a tabletop so slowly one assumes the wood has always been gray. In spring, soon after he'd moved back to the quarters provided for the farm workers, she left although she knew he would turn up on Sunday looking for her. She left before the lavender could bloom—pungent, honeyed—and seduce her into staying another season. "I will not settle for this simulacrum of love," she said aloud as she got into the car. "I will not." She was prepared to strip away the scented sheets she had used in those two years to shroud her past. Beneath the placid surface of the fields, beneath the delicate rows of green that surrounded her house, she knew things were seething—earthworms chewing up the soil, ants tunneling, maggots feasting on the corpse of a bird. As she drove off, she saw the cypresses in the rearview mirror and realized she'd planted them for more than shade: they made the house seem like the great stone gate to a tomb and so had allowed people passing by to read, with clarity, the state of mind of its inhabitant.

Three, three-thirty, quarter to four. The clock's luminous dial marks time with a circle of clicks. Listen, count the tick-tick-tick. Stop tossing and try to lie still, hands crossed neatly and growing numb. Out on the avenue, don't you hear the sirens wail? If you go to the window, you'll see them spiral by, reflected in the wet pavement. What else can you make out down at the end of this narrow block? Some rodent scurrying along the gutter. The neon pinks and yellows of the donut shop, bar, and all-night delicatessen, and the black shapes of customers walking into the lights. In a different life we walked along there— remember—bought milk, a pack of cigarettes, a tube of ointment for stiff joints. We'd watch the mechanical display figures jerk their limbs behind the dirty glass while, inside, people raised their arms to take a box from the shelf, tightened their jaws when they saw the price. You claim now that you hated those expeditions, that you would rather have stayed home, but you used to like to tip your head back from the confines of the gray buildings and fire escapes and look up at the pale spring sky. Mad cries bounced from the barred windows.

It's no use trying to rest in this small room the color of lead. Night presses down, no way to dislodge the weight. Get up then, shuffle from chair

*to door and back again. Wrap the Spanish shawl
tightly around your shoulders. Perambulate.
Think of other walks taken when we could walk
more than ten steps without tiring, other rooms
lived in by you or somebody else. There on the
table with its ruffled cloth sit photos we never
look at and the radio we never listen to, switched
off in the middle of a symphony years ago. I know
you; you think the mind is enough. Blood pulses
through arteries and capillaries to the brain like
a string of bulbs firing in turn on a theater's mar-
quee. The play can proceed, interrupted only by
the clatter of the furnace: a rumbling speech,
broken voices, a withering script you might not
escape from. Outside, the wind has settled for the
night but the signs still flicker off and on in con-
cert. Another group of sirens flashes by, signaling
someone's death by gun, fire, or brittle heart. Or
birth.*

IV

The man had hair long and bitter as the afternoon
storms, a reach wider than the river, skin like the
rotten leaves beneath a log, breath hotter and
damper than the air under the densest part of the
jungle canopy. The island that kept her sat in a
stream of brown water; the banks were far away
but if she pressed the branches aside, she could
sometimes see people picnicking on the strip of
bare ground under the bridge, eating Ring-Dings,
bananas, and manioc bread, that much closer to
civilization. She parted the creepers—quickly,
quietly—just enough so she could see them but
they couldn't see her. The man hadn't yet put a
price on looking out, though as she'd learned early
on, there was a high one on speaking out: she had

called and waved to a boat, sure that some pas-
senger or crewman would hear her without too
much fuss, when he jumped and knocked her
down, striking his claws through her shoulders.
"Now dearest," he hissed while she tried to catch
her breath, "you shouldn't go showing yourself
like that." Inside his wide, pink mouth the teeth
were sharp and wet, his palate rippled. He dragged
her to the interior where the ground was clear of
underbrush and the light among the tree trunks
was a palpable sickening green. After sitting her
down in the cagelike roots of a pandanus palm,
he pried a stone from the earth with the same
concentration as a boy picking a splinter from
his foot, then carved and heated it and applied
it to her skin, the pain so keen she could see
the brand's intricate design—a snake squirming
around a flowering branch—in her mind's eye
before she had a chance to inspect the wound, a
bright red weal on her bruised thigh, just the colors of the orchids drooping above her like diseased
tongues. There, at the dead center of the island, he
allowed her to scream all she wanted and stepped
back into the shadows, changing color and dis-
sipating like a gas. She smelled him: invisible,
everywhere.

Long ago, he'd taken her as bounty. He'd swal-
lowed her; one of the trees had opened and then
closed again. When she straightened from his
grasp, he saw she was slender, young, her skin's
pale bluish cast. "Let me go," she'd shrilled, but
he covered her mouth and wedged her under a
fallen log. "You're mine now," he whispered
while she watched her family search, and at dusk
give up the search. "A nice prize," he thought,
wondering how much trouble she would be. She

heard her father say that they'd come back, but they were never able to approach the island again, a new current having developed, overnight it seemed. From the hiding place he'd made for her, she watched them paddling the canoes toward the shore only to be deflected again and again; she watched until one day they didn't appear and she realized they must have thought she was dead.

In some ways, it was a life of ease. He served her meals of fruits, vegetables, and raw fish and cleaned up afterwards. Gently, he anointed her with his own special preparation to keep the ants away. And when she woke with a bouquet of spiny pink bromeliads and red passion flowers by her head, she almost felt tempted to accept this fate. Much more often though, she told herself she could leave on her own, push through the giant lily pads, brave caimans, crocodiles and anacondas, and wade across to the east bank or the west; it made little difference as each, with its wall of green vegetation, its tangle of bushes, ferns and vines, its loud chick-chick and buzz of invisible insects, was a replica of the island shores. "I can do it. Just you wait and see," she'd yell and he'd answer with an almost human laugh. She was determined not to give up. In the middle of a wild storm or on a still heat-stroke morning so brilliant the man would not dare to come out of the shade, she'd try for the strip of dirt under the bridge, swim-float there, crawl up, and beg for a towel. Or, on a hot damp moonless night when the surrounding hills were only silhouettes and the cars went by on the bridge like another breeze in the leaves, she could call for help from the water beneath the roadway. But the river creatures were fierce, and the stones around the island were excruciatingly sharp; she knew as she had waded out a number of times trying to reach clear water where she could wash off the mud and sooth bites and scratches without being afraid of leeches. Each time, the man came to bring her back as if they were playing an elaborate game of hide-and-seek. The rocks didn't seem to bother him, and he scooped her up in his arms as if he were the river itself washing her onto the bank.

Other days she felt less defiant. "What I need is a rescuer," she thought as she stared up at the blue sky that perfectly fill the canyon the river cut through the jungle, "a whole rescue party of men and women with portable radios, candy, a bar of soap, and a new red dress." She thought of this in the early evening when she wandered the island, scraping at the trees to see the underbark of gold or to smell the much-missed odor of cold roast chicken that came from the wood. When the heat was unbearable, tight as a strangling fig, in the middle of the day, she lay back and dreamed about deliverance. At night after the man stifled his squawks and stilled his hands that had been busy as a spider monkey's about her, once he loosened the knots in the lianas and left her alone to flick off the bloody bodies of the mosquitoes that had been crushed between them, she dreamed of a dress of soft red cotton with flounces, a tight bodice, and a sash; she realized the only way she'd get that dress would be with the utmost patience. She felt him behind every tree. He guarded her too well for anyone to get through. In those dark moments when it was impossible to sleep, she tried to find consolation in the thought that she was younger than he. Perhaps if nothing else worked, he would die before her and his death would set her free: the currents would return to their original courses, beasts would disappear from the waters and shores, the stones on the river bottom would turn to sand. As she fell asleep, she thought she glimpsed the brilliant blue of a bird of paradise that had torn through the thick canopy of leaves so that she could grab on to its curlicued tail and be gone.

When she'd been just a bit younger, she'd dreamed of a love like a South Sea isle, warm as a lagoon ringed with coral and as insular. When she'd arrived on this island, she'd cried from pain and humiliation, mourned the things she couldn't have. Now she only thought of the cars on the bridge, or rather, once one passed and she recognized the screech of tires at a sharp bend in the road and got a whiff of exhaust, she thought, dry-eyed and furious, how she'd missed her chance again, cursed herself for her fear of the man's stiff puttylike hands clamping down on her from behind.

V

The marble bench floated in the middle of the room like the slab of a sarcophagus on a pale lake, its molded edges slapped by shadows. On the green walls: paintings in gilt frames. A man's shoes squeaked rhythmically. He paced in front of Titian's *Venus and the Lute Player* with his hands clasped behind his back, stopped, took off his raincoat and draped it elegantly over his arm, breathed deeply, regained his composure. After straightening his tie, he walked over to a woman scribbling in a notebook, her shoulders hunched. Oblivious, Veronese's angels flew in a realm of blue. The man and woman talked, walked back to the Titian together, right up to it. No one had touched that painting with a bare hand since the artist himself.

"The oddest thing just happened to me." He wanted to convince her but he didn't know how. He thought that, perhaps, she might love him for this. "I was looking at that painting, Titian's Venus. Want to come over there with me?" He looked down at her small mouth set in a hesitant smile.

"He's crazy," she thought, "the way his eyes flicker wildly." She tried to study her notes, to chew her pencil, but he didn't stop staring. "He wants me to follow him," she thought.

Pretty, curvaceous—he was already thinking that way, thinking what it would be like to hold her. But mostly he wanted to tell her what had happened to him. The goddess spoke to him. Crazy. What should he do? Who should he tell? Her: she was the only one there. He offered her his arm, hoping she'd take it.

"Harmless," she told herself. "But talk to strangers? To me?" Was he trying to pick her up? She'd walk over to the painting with him, then see what happened. Perhaps he'd turn out to be charming; he was tall, gray-haired, and slender, after all. His hands shook though, like windshield wipers hanging loosely in front of his body. A few steps ahead, he was waiting for her.

The two people danced forward, she slower than he, in a polonaise, minuet, fandango. At the Titian she stood a bit behind him.

"She's wonderful, wonderful," he said. "I come every weekend to see her. That voluptuous landscape. She's staring out of the frame at her lover."

She had a belly like a melon, mushy and lopsided. She lay around naked, showing off her fleshy arms and pudgy useless fingers. Her nipples looked like pencil erasers. What was she doing there with this man? She had her work to think about. Cupid reached up to put a garland of pink flowers on Venus's blond head, and the man laughed, a cross between a wheeze and a chuckle, a quick intake of breath popped out again in spurts. Should she laugh too? She felt silly. He was an absolute stranger.

With his pinkie, he pointed to the details, wondering how to get to the important information. He smelled rose water. It came from Venus, didn't it? He liked it very much. "The lute player—why is he wearing that black velvet hat and cape on such a hot day? Everyone else is naked. Venus only has pearls in her hair." Even though he wanted to know if she was paying attention, he avoided looking at her.

"Yes, I can see that."

The man twisted his head around, in the woman's general direction, but she seemed to keep slipping out of his sight. He had to twist further and further. "Look at the way the musician strains his neck to stare at her when it would be so much easier for him just to look at the scenery. Why doesn't he?" He tried to say this rationally. He was afraid that if he looked directly at her, turned his whole body, he'd find she was making faces at him. Of course, if he did look at her, she would probably stop. Out of politeness.

A very strange sight: in a room devoted to sixteenth-century Italian painting, a man screwed his head around backwards. His body faced one wall while he managed to look at the opposite. Next to him, a woman stood, nodding and staring down. The floor washed up against the walls as if the outside world—the river, the bay, then the ocean—had entered: vertigo.

She held her breath because she didn't want to look at the painting anymore. She wanted to get away but she didn't know how. This relationship had already gone on for too long. Could she say that she had to return to her note-taking because she had to write a paper for the next day? She didn't think he'd believe her. She didn't think he'd believe any excuse.

He had to tell her, not let her escape. Perhaps it would be better if he turned to her again. He unwound his neck with a creak. "An old trick," he laughed. The skin on her eyelids was oily, translucent. Underneath, he could see her eyes moving around. If she walked off, he would follow her. It must have been fate that brought them together, meant for each other; soon Cupid would pull an arrow from the quiver, fit it to his bow.

An ordinary man, rather debonair, and a younger woman studied a painting by Titian or by the school of Titian. Beyond the loggia, there were mounds of reddish brown dirt, a group of naked people dancing under the trees, minute swans in a watercourse, and a haze of blue atmospheric mountains fading into the sky.

She was afraid that, in order to get away from him, she'd have to leave the museum altogether and go home to her cramped apartment, walk down the narrow streets with the heavy, already dark sky throwing itself on her back. No, she'd rather stay. "Maybe he'll get tired of this soon," she thought. "They're calling for more rain tomorrow," she said as he'd been very quiet for some time. "It's lovely there in the painting."

She was coming round. He could talk to her

after all. "Can you imagine if it rained there?" he asked, pointing to the picture. He imagined a fine warm velvety mist. "They'd get drenched. They only have those red curtains to protect them."

His chuckle sounded evil. "Crazy." She forced a laugh, and he moved a little closer. "A mistake to laugh," she thought. He smiled secretively and jingled his keys in the pocket of his gray tweed trousers. She watched him carefully, pretending not to.

"Have you noticed anything strange about the painting yet?" He thought Cupid might have turned toward them slightly but since she shook her head, he added, "I'll just let you look for a while longer then." He felt himself calming down, yearned for heat though, yearned to wrap himself in the canvas as if in a blanket. He was happy he'd gotten up his nerve to talk to her, nervously awaited her reply. "I've seen her here before. In this very room," he thought. He felt sure she'd smiled at him when he'd come in and was sorry he hadn't responded right away. She'd obviously been hurt but he'd make her forget that now.

Inside the frame the paint glittered like a body of water in the sun—flat, vertical. Even the hot sky full of magnificent billowing clouds glittered. Through the false skylight the bulbs shed an incandescent white.

"You still haven't seen anything?" He was getting impatient again, shifting his weight from one foot to the other.

"Well," she said, afraid, "the landscape almost seems to hang behind the people like a tapestry, like they could reach out and touch it." She heard her voice rising, questioning. She'd wanted to sound sure of herself, to intimidate him into shutting up. When he thrust his arm out as if to stick it through the painting, she caught his wrist.

"Ridiculous," he said, shaking free. "Ridiculous. How can you say such a thing? Just look at that landscape; it goes on forever. You're just like her, ignoring it completely." He grunted. "It's as if the only reason she's out of doors at all is that the maids are busy doing the rooms. And when that landscape is just as tempting as she is too." He breathed rapidly, heavily.

She backed away though he had her hand now and was trying to draw her nearer. "Strength," she told herself and waited for him to relax. "But what was so odd then? " she asked once his grip on her had weakened. "What happened to you? Tell me already."

"You don't really want to hear," he said.

"Yes, yes, of course I do."

He stared at his hands and began slowly. "She talked to me, Venus I mean." He said it as matter-of-factly as possible, jerked his head toward the painting. His whole body was trembling, inside to out. "She said, 'Come here,' and I knew she was talking to me because you were at the other end of the room. I thought I imagined it at first, but she nodded to encourage me and gestured with her hand, the one holding the recorder." Pacing again, he'd thought he'd feel relieved but he only felt crazier, anxious. His palms began to sweat.

By the bench, two figures stood on the blond floor: she motionless while he turned around her. What began as a stately walk became a whirlpool.

He made her dizzy. "Mad." Who knew what he would do if she laughed? Besides, she felt a bit sorry for him now that she could see how he twitched and shook, tugged at his hair, gnawed his fingernails. "Perhaps you did imagine it," she suggested. "The light in here isn't very good."

"No, no, no," he said. He felt himself losing her. He'd been right; he shouldn't have told a soul, but now that he'd started. . . ."You see how the frame cuts off the bottom of the scene right in the middle of that viola da gamba? The separation between art and life is quite accidental, quite tenuous, you see." Grabbing her tiny shoulders, he pulled her closer. He'd make her realize that what he said was true. "I thought about trying to step onto the loggia. Really I did, but the painting's hung too high. I'd have to grab on and haul myself in." He stopped and stared at Venus but her smile hadn't changed. "I was welcome there anyway."

Disentangling herself, she stepped away and was surprised he didn't follow. "Do you want my help? Is that it? I could give you a boost, I suppose." She felt a bit tremulous. Her shoulder still hurt, but she thought, gratefully, that this was almost over now. Perhaps he'd forgotten her, he was so quiet. He shook his head like a dog hearing a high-pitched whistle.

"No, no." He turned suddenly and knew if he didn't leave that second, he would start to moan and cry. She pitied him now, too much. Running down the wide central staircase, he thought of her back there, her flowered skirt, the birds on her sweater flying against the lovely clouds of her body, Venus's eyes. He couldn't go back until she was gone.

In the green-walled room: hissing of heat, slight crackle and buzz of electric light. The floor seemed to tip and tilt until the woman felt she had to sit down. From the bench she stared at the irregular opening between the velvet curtains onto the lush and beautiful world beyond. She traveled back, back, back into the distant blue and gold haze until the image of that country imprinted itself on her retina. For the rest of her life, she saw the world through a scrim of Venus and lute player the way others see through cigarette smoke or rose-colored glasses. She believed that this made her life more pleasant, that it protected her from loneliness, but one day she walked out into the middle of traffic on Park Avenue thinking it was an open loggia.

VI

"Walk," he said. "Just keep walking."

She walked even though she thought it was crazy, wondered why she had come out in the middle of this wintry night. She wished she had worn other shoes and her heavy jacket too. "Don't think about it," she kept telling herself. After a little while she stopped to rest, hoping he wouldn't notice, hoping he'd keep on without her and she could return to the car. She still had the keys. Across the road red and blue spotlights shone on an office building, throwing lines of deep shadow on the windows. Rubber plants, bamboo and palm trees stood guard inside the lobby doors. No one was around.

"You stopped," he said. "Don't stop walking. I want to show you this spot at dawn." Next to her, he hulked in the dark.

"My feet hurt and I'm cold."

"Stop complaining. You agreed to come. Why did you come anyway?"

She thought of saying "Because you're pointing a gun at me, you fool," but she played dumb instead, stamping her feet on the pavement to keep the blood going, trying not to let him see she was scared. "We've been friends a long time and you asked me to. Something seemed wrong."

"Nothing's wrong. I just wanted to come for a walk here. No one ever walks here. Now let's get going." He gripped her arm tightly above the elbow and pushed her along with his thigh so that she stumbled in the cinders and gravel.

Around them the land rolled slightly, waves of black earth studded with blast furnaces and smelters. She felt her pulse jump where he was holding her and tried to think about mazes of pipes and conduits, high temperatures, petroleum products, and the weird yellow color of the sky in order to keep from thinking about anything else.

He had turned up on her doorstep at two in the morning, and while she talked, stared down the street where the lights at the kitchen doors were spaced evenly as beacons. The whole time, he'd held his hand in his coat pocket, a little away from his body the way hit men do in the movies, black and white slitting their faces in half. When he'd asked her to go, she'd put on her shoes and followed him to the car. He made her drive, not telling her where they were going, just when to turn and where to stop.

"Am I being abducted?" she asked. She'd read somewhere that many crime victims know their assailants. Bert had some money to rescue her with. "He could mortgage the house," she thought.

"I'm not kidnapping you. Don't be silly," he said and stopped, pulled her around to face him. Lit from behind, his hair glowed wildly. His mouth opened and closed like a beak when he talked. He'd been cruel to her before but never this cruel and not for years, not since they were children and he'd commit some offense just to see her scream "Get out, get out of my house right now." He'd sit back on his heels and laugh and laugh. "I asked you to come, didn't I?"

She thought he looked grim, as if he were chewing sand, so she didn't bring up the question of her free will in the matter but started to walk down the narrow road again before he could say anything else. The wind hustled over the vast spaces, through the dark fences, around her. At the gates of the factories the guard booths stood empty, though she could hear trucks grinding their gears at the loading docks if she listened carefully. "Eventually," she thought, "one of them has to turn out onto the road and stop to ask us what we're doing here." The wind picked up again, whistling between the towers, fluctuating tones like breath drawn over the top of a bottle. On nights like this the kids curled to keep warm. If she were home, she'd be checking to make sure they hadn't thrown the blankets off in a dream the way she did. "Where are we going? Are we almost there?"

They kept on for hours though the surroundings didn't change; their feet scratched the road. Next to her, he seemed to grow stronger, taller, more silent. His hands stuck in his coat pockets, his presence was monstrous, capable of anything. The air smelled sulfurous, as if hundreds of matches had just been blown out around them, but despite the hot smell, she shivered. "What next? What next?" Whenever they approached a refinery, a factory, even a single oil tank with iron steps circling it, she strained to see over the fields of rubble or the parking lots, hoping to find the yellow rectangle of a small window. Any sign that other people were awake would do. Each time though, a white rancid light surrounded the dark blocks, a fortune in electricity but never anything on a human scale. Disappointed, she lowered her head again.

Forever, she thought, they'd walk by this power plant, by the high tension wires that buzzed between the steel pylons, under the thick black sky. Everything crackled and hummed: distributors, turbines, generators, dynamos. More than a dozen smokestacks sent up ocherous plumes that dispersed under the clouds. Flames shot from chimneys, over towers that wavered and swayed. Yes, everything moved on its own; mesmerized, she was sure of it. In a glass walkway between buildings she saw two people having a conversation and started to run. He stopped her short, though, with a sharp tug at her arm, enough pain so she wouldn't try to break free again. His hand clutched her wrist like an automaton's claw, and he pointed at the image: one look subdued her. She'd seen their own reflections, dancing because of the iridescent flames, and she kept on going now without waiting to be told, walking into a trance, one step after another, up and down hills, around bends, along an endless chain-link fence.

"I still don't know why I had to come along," she said finally, hoping he'd tell her. Now that his hand was free of the pocket bumping heavily against their legs, she felt a little safer, calmer.

"For the company, that's all," he said gruffly. She wanted to believe him.

Just before dawn, a streak of pale color cracked the sky in the east and the land spread out in front of them; a saltiness crept into the bitter air. "We must be nearing the sea," she thought dreamily.

"We'll have to stop there. I'll be able to sit on a rock, look at the blue water." It made her realize how tired she was.

"It's getting light," he said and tightened his fingers on her wrist. So he wasn't going to let her go. Was he afraid she'd leave him? "Why the hell don't I?" she wondered, "even if he does pull out the gun? Why did I come anyway?" She could have shut the door in his face after all and ducked behind the hall table in case he decided to start shooting, but she'd been willing to come. Because the mahogany whatnot and gold-framed mirror in her front hall looked suddenly like toys? Because the stripes on the wallpaper had begun to swirl? Because Bert and the children asleep upstairs paled to phantoms when she saw him standing on the porch? Or had she come with him simply to escape the all-night round of couch, bed and kitchen table, of numerous cups of warm milk with rum? If she were home, she might be dropping off to sleep just as the morning light defined that lump in the corner as a pile of laundry and touched the bush in the yard she kept meaning to trim from its ferocious shape. Here, the light defined nothing safely, worse than in the dreams she woke from whimpering, her teeth sunk into the pillow or her husband's arm.

"Here," he said softly.

The road disappeared in front of a dilapidated warehouse, its high arched roof blocking out most of the sky, its brick walls lopsided and scarred. At one end a wide ramp sloped into the swamp, and further out, the land also eased into the brown water. The tips of the marsh grasses were a pale green though. A breeze came up and stirred them, dispersed the clouds, exposed a blue sky and the low, early sun. In the building the windows burst simultaneously into flame, thirty panes of gold, bejewelled as a reliquary, leaping with color—red, orange, a reflected sapphire blue—glittering. He still gripped her wrist but she thought it felt almost like a caress, and suddenly she breathed freely. He'd even smiled. When was the last time he'd done that? It was OK, she thought, if that stretch of road was the last place in the world, if those factories on the flats were the only memorials, that it was all right if the fountains were now waste pipes sticking out over the water and the construction sites looked more like excavations. Things would get built; they'd help. Funny, she thought, how she hadn't seen him for years and then, once again, they were going to the same parties, meeting for coffee. Every one of his features had narrowed but otherwise he looked the same. He had turned up, just the way he used to appear and take her off to the railroad yard or the dump. They'd dug for old bottles there, and she'd thought she could still smell a sweet-sour tonic in them. After saving the whole ones, they smashed the pieces against a stone, throwing as if they had only one arm between them. They roared at the spatter, knelt and scooped up the shards, let the splinters stick into their palms, waited to see the spots of blood break out like measles. She'd forgotten she'd joined him in that.

He'd been staring out at the water, back down the road, but he inched closer now, standing against her so that she needed to look up at him. Feeling the heat from his body, she reached her hand out to touch him. He ignored it, though, as if he'd forgotten she was there. She noticed how tired he looked, gray, old, and felt she must look the same.

"It's quiet on that road, isn't it? " he said calmly, lightly, as if he'd just shown her a special bit of countryside or his favorite gallery in a museum, but his face was motionless. Then, as if he were stepping toward her, as if he were pushing her with his eyes, jagged and bright as glass, she backed off the roadway and into the marsh. The ground gave way under her. It could break through at any minute and let her fall. Save herself? She couldn't. She wouldn't have time. And how? Reach out for a hand as cold as ice, as cold as something already dead? No, she'd just have to pull it all with her—the whole mess of industry along the road, smokestacks, towns, every house including her own, factory flames at night putrid and gaudy as paintings on velvet, and him too. They'd sink, their breath cut short, trapped like those mammoths in Los Angeles.

Past dawn there's no reason for fear. Pull aside the curtains shut in a final and unsuccessful attempt to sleep. Outside, the sky has faded from its nighttime purple glow to gray, and the meager light flattens the view of trash cans, automobiles, shopping carts. It will rain again today, the clouds contracting then letting loose. Come, turn away; you insist on watching the day broaden and wither. Don't tell me to let you stand there, that you'll come from the window in your own good time. You never do and later complain of headaches, malaise, and a cramped neck.

She'll be here soon. Hide your robe in the closet and put on a simple brown sweater instead. Stuff jewels under the mattress and candle ends in dresser drawers. She doesn't like to see us up this early but prefers to wake us with a sharp knock that never needs to be answered because she opens the door herself, assuming we have no secrets. Crawl back into bed and balance the pad of newsprint on knees rocky and fragile, forget fatigue, set up the box of colored pencils, and with the growing light, flip page after page, making marks.

A journey. Every summer we went to a hotel a mile from the sea. There, we woke to larks and turtledoves in a room made wider with mirrors. From the pillow we looked up and saw a ring of golden fruit where the white walls and ceiling met: pineapples and grapes. French doors opened on three sides to balconies that overlooked wheat fields, forests, and asparagus beds. One railing was brushed by palm fronds, and if we leaned on another, we could see down the hill to the blue waters of the bay where sailboats heeled, dancing. Along the promenade, red flowers bloomed and ladies carried parasols made of light. Don't say you hated it. Don't tell me my memory is false. You were there too even if you say I'm only imagining a painting by Monet I've seen in a library book somewhere. You enjoyed it even if you say, now, that you felt trapped behind a screen, that you never were in contact with the world. It's true we didn't go out much. We never did get to touch the carmine petals, but the world came into our room. From the easy chair we smelled salt and wild roses. Attendants brought our cup of thick morning chocolate, our lunch of prosciutto and melon, binoculars to see the coun-

tryside up close. Here, we fill the white mug with weak coffee from an electric urn ourselves.

Lie, wait for the door to open; she'll be smiling so sweetly. Her shoes squeak on the linoleum and her hands are always warm and dry when she hooks the pink corset, helps us on with our favorite blue wool dress, the one with cut glass buttons. Then she hands us the cane and gently but firmly steers us in the direction of the dining room for breakfast, past the doors unlocked only to let visitors in, garbage out in plastic bags at bedtime. Ah, not for an hour yet. The buses are only just beginning to shuffle along, the sun to paste a yellow triangle on the brick wall opposite before the clouds gather again. Time for one last will-o'-the-wisp. Tell. Tell all.

VII

The blue diamond of the summer sky stood over the tablelands and a facet of that blue spanned the uneven hollow that contained a small, purer circle: the lake that pressed shore here, retreated from it there. Situated such, between cliffs dropping from a plateau, its water did not reflect sky or clouds, hawks, vultures, grass sprouting from the dirt, took nothing from the exterior; even the occasional thunderstorm failed to ruffle its surface. Despite high alkalinity and the growth of microorganisms, primordial groups of cells that, present more densely, would have been the color of bricks, the lake remained absolutely clear, a sheet of warmish water, serving only as a warped mirror of its own basin, a distortion of mud cracked into a pattern of itself, fissures tracing fissures in thick brown clay, no weeds, no ripples from pupfish or bubbles from worms. The water level rose and fell though, closing and disclosing, coloring and discoloring. In spring on the table-lands, gray-green sagebrush covered the ground like dust on dust, and the tips of the ocotillo's long thorny branches blazed with odorless red flowers; in summer the lake evaporated, leaving behind a sediment of silt and salt, the intricacies of crystals that grew around a point, a branching repetition that formed a white ring between the mud and the dust. Around the lake the valley rose gently and then steeply to the plateau, jagged, scraped, over-grown. No wind disturbed the place, the air was still and dead, and the heat—dry, hard—pressed against the ground the way a rock, falling slowly, squeezes space—this despite the long leap from the valley floor to the blue expanse, despite the wide stretch from horizon to horizon up on the flatlands.

Out of the clear summer sky, the whir and buzz of the plane's engine came first and then the plane itself. Dipping its wings, it expelled a long series of vapor circles, white, exhaustive. It flew—a monster, so long had it been since they'd seen such a machine. And in it: people. There must have been. The lake did not reflect spinning and circling although the surface wobbled under the stir of air and yielded to the shadow of the plane, a moving smudge of charcoal, a new color entering the scheme. What did it remind them of? They allowed this question in a landscape that permit-ted none. (Why none? Because color defined dis-tance, shadows defined objects, the heat was absolute and the shade cold without recourse.) Besides birds, pterodactyls, flies, dragons—what? But none of these, for the sun glanced off its wings as if off shards of mirror. Did they answer the question? They turned its mysteries over in their mind a few times as they stood with hat tilted back to see better, fist thumping thigh, other hand scratching chin. From the air they would be a spot on the land, unseeable for unexpected: no one lived out there, no road, no house, what fresh water? what food? what companionship? They would be less than the shadow of the plane as long as they remained still, less than the shadow of red-tailed fox or kangaroo rat. Buzz constant, the plane circled lower and higher, below the rim of the bluffs and up again, down toward the lake. Then, silence refilled the space like water breaking a dike and the plane fell, not plummeting but angling off, its momentum carrying it on after the engines failed. They fully expected it to pull up again as if the whole thing were a circus act put on for their pleasure, education, edification, but trajectory honed fine, the plane slammed into the rock just below the top of the cliff, the white shape crumpling and then ballooning into a chrysanthemum of flame. And they had to admit their training was perfect: they felt nothing—no wonder or pain, no sense of loss, no need to rush down the loose-earthed slope and along the lake shore to the site, nothing to rescue and no desire to do so, almost no curiosity, acceptance only. Had they been looking for them, their friends? They must have had friends, else why would they think the word, but they cannot recall faces or hands. Had the rush of engine into solid rock reminded them that one could still be looked for out there? They'd say no; the roar, cough, and silence had raised the possibility of this question but the flower of flame and the heat it threw across the valley had not awakened any need to answer it.

The lake rises and falls, leaving salt crystals on plane parts at shore. The shock of energy released when metal slapped stone sent one wave across the water to bounce off the opposite shore, travel back and bounce again until it cancelled itself out in the middle of the lake, dissipated. Slowly, air and water corrode the metal that's left, so slowly that the sections of wing and tail are the same every day for a long time.

If they are still again, it is because they traded pressure and energy like secrets and reached a tenuous equilibrium. They split and multiply, grow in spirals and disperse in water; they group together red as blood. The valley makes them walk with varied pace, stumbling here, jumping there, glancing down at the land and staring up at the quartzite sky. Another cycle, ageless. They've been here so very long or has it only been months, minutes, days. Each step, each boot heel in the dust, is an intrusion and a gift, a change from one thing to another, neither forward nor back.

PREVIOUS WINNERS OF THE
DRUE HEINZ LITERATURE PRIZE

The Death of Descartes, by David Bosworth, 1981
Dancing for Men, by Robley Wilson, Jr., 1982
Private Parties, by Jonathan Penner, 1983
The Luckiest Man in the World, by Randall Silvis, 1984
The Man Who Loved Levittown, by W. D. Wetherell, 1985
Under the Wheat, by Rick DeMarinis, 1986
In the Music Library, by Ellen Hunnicutt, 1987
Moustapha's Eclipse, by Reginald McKnight, 1988